BEAR TRAP

Fargo wheeled his horse past the cub as a tremendous roar resounded, and he looked back to see the monstrous mother grizzly charging at him, intent on ripping him to ribbons.

"Damn!" Fargo said, and lashed the stallion into a full-out run. In an amazing display of speed, the grizzly was actually gaining on them. Fargo goaded the Ovaro to go faster. At breakneck pace they flew through the forest, vaulting obstacles and avoiding deadfalls. Fargo looked back over his shoulder, and he couldn't believe what he was seeing.

The grizzly was twenty feet behind them. Then fifteen. Then ten.

The bear's maw opened, revealing teeth covered in frothy blood.

With a roar, the beast leapt at him. . . .

THE
TRAILSMAN
#235

FLATHEAD
FURY

by

Jon Sharpe

A SIGNET BOOK

SIGNET
Published by New American Library, a division of
Penguin Putnam Inc., 375 Hudson Street,
New York, New York 10014, U.S.A.
Penguin Books Ltd, 27 Wrights Lane,
London W8 5TZ, England
Penguin Books Australia Ltd, Ringwood,
Victoria, Australia
Penguin Books Canada Ltd, 10 Alcorn Avenue,
Toronto, Ontario, Canada M4V 3B2
Penguin Books (N.Z.) Ltd, 182–190 Wairau Road,
Auckland 10, New Zealand

Penguin Books Ltd, Registered Offices:
Harmondsworth, Middlesex, England

First published by Signet, an imprint of New American Library,
a division of Penguin Putnam Inc.

First Printing, May 2001
10 9 8 7 6 5 4 3 2 1

The first chapter of this book originally appeared in *Apache Duel*,
the two hundred thirty-fourth volume in this series.

REGISTERED TRADEMARK—MARCA REGISTRADA

Printed in the United States of America

PUBLISHER'S NOTE
This is a work of fiction. Names, characters, places, and incidents either are the product
of the author's imagination or are used fictitiously, and any resemblance to actual
persons, living or dead, business establishments, events, or locales is entirely coincidental.

BOOKS ARE AVAILABLE AT QUANTITY DISCOUNTS WHEN USED TO PROMOTE PRODUCTS OR
SERVICES. FOR INFORMATION PLEASE WRITE TO PREMIUM MARKETING DIVISION, PENGUIN
PUTNAM INC., 375 HUDSON STREET, NEW YORK, NEW YORK 10014.

The Trailsman

Beginnings . . . they bend the tree and they mark the man. Skye Fargo was born when he was eighteen. Terror was his midwife, vengeance his first cry. Killing spawned Skye Fargo, ruthless, cold-blooded murder. Out of the acrid smoke of gunpowder still hanging in the air, he rose, cried out a promise never forgotten.

The Trailsman they began to call him all across the West: searcher, scout, hunter, the man who could see where others only looked, his skills for hire but not his soul, the man who lived each day to the fullest, yet trailed each tomorrow. Skye Fargo, the Trailsman, the seeker who could take the wildness of a land and the wanting of a woman and make them his own.

*In the wilds of Montana, 1861—
one man's lust for power threatened
to unleash a bloodbath that would
stain the wilderness scarlet. . . .*

1

The big man in buckskins squinted up from under his hat brim at the bright afternoon sun. He had been in the saddle since before daybreak and looked forward to stopping for the night, but it would be another five to six hours yet.

Skye Fargo spied a golden eagle soaring high on air currents in search of prey, its wings outspread. Off among a cluster of spruce trees a jay squawked noisily and was answered by one of its kind. Much closer, almost from under the hooves of his pinto stallion, rose a rapid chittering. Fargo's lake-blue eyes lowered to a feisty chipmunk that was scolding him for daring to intrude on its domain. Dwarfed by the Ovaro, the tiny curmudgeon threw a fit, prancing and chattering in a frenzy.

Fargo smiled. He loved the wilderness. To him it was home. He knew the creatures that lived there as well as city dwellers knew their neighbors. He knew the habits of every animal, knew the sounds they made and the tracks they left. So when a faint whine fell on his ears his interest perked and he tilted his head to pinpoint the direction it came from.

It was a low, pitiable whine, such as a wolf or coyote might make. Wolves, though, were seldom abroad at that time of the day and coyotes ordinarily preferred open country to dense woodland.

Fargo veered aside to investigate. Instinctively he lowered his right hand to the smooth butt of the Colt on his hip. He doubted whatever was out there posed a threat, but it didn't pay to be careless.

The whining grew louder. The Ovaro pricked its ears but otherwise showed no alarm.

Fargo threaded through some ponderosa pines and came to a thicket. He reined wide to go around when suddenly some of the thin branches shook. Halting, he peered into the thicket's depths, not quite knowing what to expect but certainly not expecting to find what he did.

A small, scruffy mongrel was on its belly, its long hair matted and dirty, its wide eyes brimming with fear. It had an oval face, a button nose, and floppy ears. Around its neck was a leather collar to which a rope leash had been attached, and the leash was tangled fast.

"Where did you come from?" Fargo wondered aloud. To his knowledge there wasn't a town or settlement within a hundred miles. Nor had he seen any sign of an Indian village. Dismounting, he sank onto his hands and knees.

The dog whined louder and tried to back away, but it couldn't go anywhere thanks to the tangled leash.

"I won't hurt you, little one," Fargo said. Removing his hat, he turned on his side, squeezed into the thicket, and crawled forward. The mongrel trembled and whimpered as if afraid he were going to eat it. "Give me a minute and I'll have you out of here."

Easier said than done, Fargo discovered. The thicket was so dense, the branches so intertwined, he had to bend or break them to force his way deeper. Sharp tips pricked his forehead and cheeks. One nearly nicked an eye. The closer he came, the more the dog quaked, and when he was almost within reach it covered its eyes with its front paws and howled in terror.

Fargo couldn't help laughing. "You're about as brave as they come," he joked, extending his right arm as far he was able. He couldn't quite reach. Wriggling another few inches, he patted the mongrel's head to soothe it and the dog stopped howling. Before he could rescue it he had to unravel the leash, which took some doing. The thing was virtually in a knot. He pried and tugged for minutes before he loosened the rope enough to make headway.

2

The dog had lowered its paws and was watching with intent interest. It had stopped trembling but still whined pitiably every now and then.

"Almost there," Fargo said, unwinding a last loop from around a last stem. A strong jerk, and it slid free. Gripping the dog's collar, Fargo carefully pulled the animal toward him. The dog offered no resistance, not even when he slipped his other hand underneath and drew it to his chest.

"I gather you haven't eaten in a while?" Fargo commented. The poor mongrel was literally skin and bones, as frail as a newborn and as weak as a kitten. It looked up, whimpered, wagged its thin tail, and licked his cheek.

"Forget it," Fargo said a bit more gruffly than he intended. "The last thing I need is a pet." Sliding out of the thicket, he stepped to the stallion and rummaged inside his saddlebags for a bundle of jerked buffalo meat he had obtained at a trading post in the Wind River country. Unwrapping the strip of hide the meat was in, he selected a piece and held the it under the dog's nose. "How about something to eat?"

The dog took one sniff and bit at the meat like a rattler striking a mouse. It was famished, and in its eagerness it accidentally nipped Fargo's finger deep enough to draw blood. After chomping furiously and greedily gulping, it eagerly gazed up at him, awaiting more.

"You can eat as we go," Fargo proposed. After retrieving his hat, he stepped into the stirrups, safely nestled his newfound companion across his saddle in front of him, and rode northward. For the next half an hour he continued to feed the starved animal morsel after morsel until only a few were left. By then the mongrel's eyelids were drooping and it could barely hold its head up.

Swiveling, Fargo stuffed what was left of the jerky back into his saddlebags. "Rest a while," he said, rubbing the dog behind its ears. "You're safe now." Hardly were the words out of his mouth than the dog slumped in exhaustion and drifted into deep slumber.

Fargo separated the leash from the collar. Whoever tied it

had used four large, rather crude knots. As the last came undone he noticed a pair of initials someone had stitched in the leather: *JJ* Did they stand for the dog's name, he wondered, or for the owner's?

The sun dipped lower in the western sky. Fargo saw no evidence of a homestead or a ranch, no sign of anything that would explain the dog's presence in the middle of nowhere. He was beginning to think that maybe the mongrel had wandered from a passing wagon train even though he wasn't anywhere near any of the trails they regularly used. Then he emerged from the forest into a broad clearing on the crest of a sawtooth ridge and spotted a cluster of buildings in a lush valley below.

Fargo had heard nothing about there being a settlement in that area. Many miles to the east there were a few, and to the south a couple had recently sprouted, but the country in the vicinity of the southern end of Flathead Lake was supposed to be virgin territory, unspoiled by human hands. It was why he was there. He wanted some time to himself, wanted to camp out by the lake for a week or two and not see another human soul.

Drawing rein, Fargo studied the buildings. He counted over two dozen arrayed along a single dusty street. Scores of cattle grazed the surrounding grassland. The sight was depressing. Each year more and more pilgrims flocked west; each year more and more of the frontier was eaten away.

"We might as well see if anyone owns you," Fargo said to the sleeping dog, and lightly touched his spurs to the Ovaro.

Deadfalls delayed their descent. It was a full forty-five minutes before Fargo neared the bottom of the slope and heard the distinctive thud of an ax striking wood. He reined toward the source.

A man in a straw hat and a boy of eight or nine, both dressed in store-bought clothes, were near the tree line. The boy was watching the man chop down a sapling. Father and son, Fargo reckoned, moving closer. Beyond the tree line a wagon had been parked, and a similarly dressed stocky townsman was stacking downed saplings in the wagon bed.

Neither the father nor his son noticed the Ovaro until it was almost on top of them. "You're lucky I'm not a hostile," Fargo said, bringing the stallion to a stop.

Both spun in alarm. The man hiked the ax to protect himself while the boy bounded behind him and peeked out.

"I don't mean you any harm," Fargo assured them. "I'm on my way to the settlement yonder. Does it have a name?"

"That it does, mister," the man found his voice. He had a haggard look about him, as if he hadn't slept well in a while. "It's called Wolfrik." He spelled the name. "Named after the man who founded it."

"The duke," the boy chimed in, A freckle-faced stringbean, he smiled shyly and admired the pinto.

"Duke?" Fargo repeated.

The man nodded. "Duke Otto Wolfrik. He moved here from a small country called Transia about two years ago." His tone implied he wasn't very fond of Wolfrik's founder.

"He lives in a great big house," the boy added, pointing to the north. "Biggest house I ever did see. It has more rooms than all the homes in Wolfrik put together."

"Is that a fact?" Fargo said. It didn't surprise him. In recent years wealthy Europeans had shown a keen interest in the untamed lands west of the Mississippi. Many had hired noted scouts to guide them on tours of the prairie and the Rockies. Some liked it so much they decided to stay and invested heavily in land.

The man lowered the ax. He had a frank, honest air about him, typical of hardworking settlers everywhere. "Where's my manners? I'm Frank Seaver. I run the general store. This here is my son, Johnny. We're cutting down trees to build a corral."

"The duke let us!" Johnny said cheerfully.

"Let you?" Fargo didn't see where Otto Wolfrik had any say in the matter. It was a free country, as the saying went, and a man could build himself a corral whenever he wanted.

Frank motioned at the wagon. "Let me introduce you to my friend. He's the town blacksmith."

Fargo lifted the reins.

"Pa, look!" Johnny abruptly bawled. "There's Jenny's dog!"

The shout woke the mongrel, which raised its head and sleepily regarded the pair. "Do you know who he belongs to?" Fargo asked.

Frank answered. "Jenny Jeeter. Her mother gave it to her for her birthday a while back. They named him Samson."

"He up and disappeared about five days ago," young Johnny revealed. "Jenny was worried sick. We looked all over, but couldn't find him anywhere."

"I came on him about five miles back," Fargo said. "Had to pry him out of a thicket."

"Five miles?" Frank said, his brow knitting. "That's awful peculiar. He never strays from Jenny's side."

"Not ever," Johnny echoed.

"There's a first time for everything. Maybe he wandered off and got lost," Fargo said. Dogs did it all the time. "I'm on my way into town. I'll drop him off when I get there."

Father and son swapped glances. "You're going into Wolfrik?" Frank asked. "There's not much there worth bothering over. If you want, Johnny and I will be more than happy to take Samson in with us and you can go on about your own business."

"I don't mind," Fargo responded. He planned to treat himself to a drink or three and maybe sit in on a few hands of poker.

The stocky man who had been loading saplings into the bed of the wagon came toward them. His store-bought shirt fit too snugly, accenting immensely muscular shoulders and an extremely thick neck. At the sight of Fargo he stopped short. "What do we have here?"

Fargo introduced himself.

"He found Jenny's dog!" Johnny exclaimed.

"Mr. Fargo, this is Luke Barstow," Frank said. "He was one of the first to move to Wolfrik."

"Lucky me," Barstow said, growling the words like an angry beast. "If I'd had any sense I'd have stayed in St.

Louis." He came toward the stallion, a brawny hand outstretched. "Give the dog to me. We'll see that it gets to its rightful owner."

"He says he wants to take Samson in himself," Frank volunteered.

Luke Barstow stopped. "That won't do. You know he can't." Walking to the pinto, Barstow reached for the mongrel's collar.

Fargo couldn't understand what the fuss was about. All he was doing was returning a lost dog. Resting his hand on Samson, he said, "I've brought him this far, I'll take him the rest of the way."

"No, you won't," Barstow persisted, and crooked a thick finger. "Hand him over. Then light a shuck and don't ever show your face in these parts again."

"I'll show my face any damn place I please," Fargo said, annoyed by the blacksmith's gall. He went to ride off but Barstow unexpectedly gripped the stallion's bridle and held on tight.

"Make this easy on yourself, mister. Strangers aren't welcome in Wolfrik. Take my advice and leave while you still can."

"Take *my* advice and mind your own affairs." Sliding his foot from the stirrup, Fargo kicked Barstow's wrist hard enough to force the blacksmith to let go. "And keep your hands off my horse."

Luke Barstow sighed. Then, without any warning whatsoever, he seized Fargo by the ankle and heaved with all his considerable might.

Fargo was upended. He experienced the sensation of falling and felt a jarring impact when his shoulder met the ground. He was up in an instant, raging mad. Samson, unfazed, was still perched on the saddle, slumped in fatigue.

The blacksmith came around the pinto toward him. "I wish there were another way," he said, and waded in with both his massive fists flying.

Granite knuckles clipped Fargo on the chin before he could

7

raise his arms to defend himself It was only a glancing blow but it rocked him on his boot heels. Almost too late he blocked an uppercut that would have shattered his jaw had it landed. He ducked another blow, sidestepped a jab, and backpedaled to buy time to clear his head. Trading punches was out of the question. The burly blacksmith was undeniably stronger and would wear him down. He had to rely on his wits and speed.

A fist arced at Fargo's face. Dodging it, he flicked a combination that did more harm to his fingers than it did to Barstow. The man's jaw was iron. So were his ribs. Fargo drove a flurry into the blacksmith's gut but it was like hitting a washtub. In skipping back he was too slow and paid for his oversight with a smashing blow to the shoulder that staggered him.

Barstow chose that moment to pause. "I don't want to do this. Agree to ride on and stay shy of Wolfrik and I'll stop. What do you say?"

Fargo let his fists reply. He struck the blacksmith on the left cheek, a solid hook that made Barstow blink, and followed through with a looping right that caught Barstow on the temple. Most men would have collapsed on the spot, but the blacksmith merely shook his head and plunged in again.

To Fargo it made no sense. Here they were, fighting for the most ridiculous of reasons. They were acting more like a pair of rowdy drunks than two grown, sober men.

Spinning to avoid a right cross, Fargo glimpsed Frank and Johnny Seaver. Both were rooted in place. Frank made no attempt to stop the fight before someone was gravely hurt. Johnny opened his mouth to shout something but Frank grasped the boy's wrist and shook his head.

A punch to the chest reminded Fargo to keep his mind on what he was doing. He blocked another jab, shifted, landed two jabs of his own, shifted once more, and drove a fist into the blacksmith's side just below the rib cage. Barstow grunted, grimaced in pain, and stopped swinging.

Now it was Fargo who paused. "Quit now, while you still can." He had no real desire to hurt the man. "Let me ride on before you regret it."

"Would that I could, mister," Luke Barstow said. Hunching low, he shot forward like a steam engine. His left shoulder slammed into Fargo's stomach even as his tree-trunk arms wrapped around Fargo's waist and bodily lifted him off the ground.

It happened so swiftly Fargo couldn't avoid the other's rush. He smashed a fist against the man's skull but it had no more effect than would a mosquito.

"Look out!" Johnny Seaver cried.

Fargo glanced over his shoulder. Barstow was about to ram him into several closely spaced saplings. Clamping an arm around the blacksmith's neck, he levered upward and to the left, throwing his entire weight into the swing, much like a cowboy would do when bulldogging a calf. His intention was to throw Barstow off balance, and he succeeded.

The blacksmith stumbled. He tried to recover but tripped and fell onto a knee, almost dragging Fargo down with him.

Tensing his hands so they were as rigid as boards, Fargo slapped them against Barstow's ears. Crying out, Barstow released him, and Fargo capitalized with three rapid uppercuts to the jaw delivered with all the force he could muster.

For a moment nothing happened. Then the blacksmith's brown eyes rolled back in their sockets and with a loud groan he pitched to the grass.

Frank Seaver was flabbergasted. "I don't believe it! No one has ever beaten Luke before."

"Thanks for trying to stop him," Fargo muttered. Rubbing a sore spot on his chin, he moved to the Ovaro. Samson was dozing, undisturbed by the violence. The saddle creaked as he hooked the horn and pulled himself up. "Be seeing you," he said to the boy, and reined the stallion toward the valley.

"Wait!" Frank said. "I hope there's no hard feelings. Believe it or not, Luke only had your best interests at heart."

"Sure he did," Fargo said. "I just hope everyone in Wolfrik isn't as crazy as the two of you." Clucking to the pinto, he cantered out of the trees and off across the tall grass. He didn't look back even when Seaver hollered.

Fargo needed that drink more than ever. He was battered and sore and simmering at how he had been treated. And all over a little dog! "What makes you so important?" he said, patting Samson's side.

A line of bent stems showed the route the wagon had taken. Soon Fargo came to a rutted road. To the right it meandered toward Wolfrik, to the left it wound off to the southeast. He turned toward town.

An air of newness clung to Wolfrik. The plank buildings were clean and tidy, the windows sparkled, the signs bore no evidence of age or fading. At the near end of the street was a three-story building that bore the largest sign of all. It was THE WOLFRIK HOTEL the sign proclaimed, *THE FINEST IN THE TERRITORY*.

Only a few people were out and about. An old man sat in an oak chair on the hotel porch, whittling. A pair of middle-aged women were strolling down the boardwalk, chatting up a storm. A portly man in a derby hat and suit was leaning against a post, reading a newspaper. On hearing the *clomp* of the Ovaro's heavy hooves they all turned, and promptly froze. Then the taller of the women said something to the other and the pair spun and made for a nearby house as if their feet were on fire. The man in the derby retreated into a store.

That left the oldster on the porch, who grinned as Fargo brought the stallion to a stop next to an empty hitch rail.

"Howdy, stranger. It isn't often anyone passes through these parts." He studied Fargo a moment from under a floppy hat. "You *are* just passing through, aren't you?"

"Friendly town you've got here," Fargo commented. Snatching the dog, he slid down. Pale faces peeked at him from nearby windows and farther down the long street a couple of men stared at him from a doorway.

"You won't find any friendlier," the old man declared. He had full, ruddy cheeks and a bushy beard that spilled over his chest halfway to his stout waist. Leaning forward, he said softly, "But if I were you, I'd get back on that hurricane deck and ride like the wind."

Fargo was tired of being told what he should do. "I'll leave when I'm good and ready." Looping the reins around the rail, he asked, "Where would I find Jenny Jeeter?"

"Widow Jeeter runs the millinery," the old man said. "Fifth building down on this side of the street. You can't miss it." He paused. "If'n you don't mind my being so nosy, are you kin of theirs by any chance?"

"I have something that belongs to them," Fargo said, and held out Samson.

"Oh. I didn't recognize the rascal. My eyes ain't what they used to be." The old man resumed whittling. "Jenny will be right pleased to see him. But you'd have done her a bigger favor by leaving the dog wherever you found him. Her heart will be broken when he disappears the next time."

"He makes a habit of it, does he?" Fargo asked.

"You'd have to ask the Jeeters. They'd know better than me. Not that it matters much. It's not who owns the dog but who owns the owners."

Fargo decided the oldster was as crazy as the blacksmith. Spurs jangling, he walked past the Wolfrik General Store, the Wolfrik Barber Shop and the Wolfrik Boot and Shoe Emporium. Scanning the other signs, he discovered every last establishment was named after the founder. Which was strange. In most towns, businesses were named after their owners.

The Wolfrik Millinery was in a frame house painted white with yellow trim. A picket fence bordered a small yard.

As Fargo opened the door a tiny bell tinkled, and the fragrant scent of lavender tingled his nose. Hats and bonnets lined a dozen shelves and were displayed on stands. A matron in a prim black dress was trying on a somber gray bonnet assisted by a much younger woman, a ravishing blonde in a blue dress that barely contained her more-than-ample bosom. Both looked over at him. The matron's mouth pinched in disapproval, but the blonde's creased in a warm smile.

"Good afternoon, sir. I'm Mary Jeeter. I'll be with you as soon as I'm finished with Mrs. McGillicutty."

Fargo had been holding Samson close to his side. Now he

11

showed the dog to her, saying, "Take your time. I'm here to drop off something that belongs to you." He thought the mother would be overjoyed to have her daughter's pet back safe and sound, but to his amazement Mary Jeeter recoiled as if she had been slapped, and pressed a hand to her bosom in stark dismay. "This is your dog, isn't it?"

"My daughter's, yes, but—" Before Mary could go on, a girl of twelve or so bustled from a side door carrying a hat box.

"I found the one you wanted, Ma."

Jenny Jeeter was the spitting image of Mary, with the same luxurious blond hair, finely chiseled face, and sparkling green eyes. She spotted Fargo and stopped so abruptly she nearly tripped over her own feet. "Samson!" she screeched. Dropping the hatbox, she flew across the room and scooped the dog into her arms. "You're alive! You're alive!"

Fargo watched the girl lavish kisses and hugs on the animal, which responded by vigorously wagging its tail and licking her face from forehead to chin in an excess of canine devotion. "At least someone is glad to see him," he remarked.

"What do you mean?" Jenny asked, glancing up. "I love Samson more than anything! Everyone told me he was dead, that I'd never see him again. But I knew better. I prayed and prayed, and look!" She gave the dog another hug. "God answered my prayers."

Mary Jeeter had recovered her composure and came toward them, moving with a fluid, sensual grace that accented her feminine charms. The enticing sway of her hips reminded Fargo of how long it had been since last he savored a woman's intimate company. "Forgive me," she said, and introduced herself and her daughter. "We're extremely grateful for what you've done, Mister . . . ?"

Fargo gave his name, and they shook. Her hand was warm and soft to the touch. That, and the musky scent of her perfume kindled a familiar hunger.

"We'd like to repay your kindness," Mary offered. "Would you accept money?"

"No," Fargo said. The little girl's happiness was reward enough.

"Invite him to supper, Ma," Jenny suggested. "Everyone says what a great cook you are."

"They exaggerate," Mary said. "And maybe Mr. Fargo wants to get on his way before dark sets in."

"I'm in no great hurry," Fargo said. The truth was, now that he had met her, he really wasn't. "I haven't had a home-cooked meal in ages."

The matron materialized beside them. She poked Fargo in the chest with a gnarled finger and hissed, "You're making a mistake, young man. Mark my words. Leave Wolfrik before it's too late!"

2

Skye Fargo couldn't recollect ever running into so many unfriendly people in one town at one time in his entire life. "Suppose you tell me just why I'll regret it?" he asked Mrs. McGillicutty.

"Outsiders have no business here. They're not welcome, and it's downright unhealthy for them to stick around."

Her logic eluded Fargo. "If you don't want outsiders, why have a hotel? And what about all the other businesses?" He nodded at the assortment of hats on the shelves. "This one, for instance. You can't tell me they only cater to townsfolk." The notion was preposterous.

"I've had my say," Mrs. McGillicutty stated, opening the door. "Whether you heed my advice is up to you. Just be careful. Beware the Blues."

"The what?" Fargo asked, but she brushed out of there as if he was afflicted with plague and she was deathly afraid of catching it. He faced the Jeeters. "Would one of you mind telling me what that was all about?"

The girl made as if to answer, but her mother put a restraining hand on her shoulder. "You heard Mrs. McGillicutty. Some people hereabouts don't like strangers much, is all," Mary said. "Please don't take it personally, but you really would be wise to move on."

"And pass up that meal?" Fargo shook his head. "Not on your life. What time do you want me here?"

Mary consulted a wall clock. "It's five-thirty now. How about seven? I don't close my shop until six and it will take a while to fire up the stove."

Fargo touched his hat brim. "See you then." He smiled at Jenny, who was cradling Samson, and went out. The matron was long gone, but waiting at the front gate was the old man from the hotel, still whittling on a block of wood. "What the hell do you want?" Fargo inquired none too politely.

"I figured you got the wrong impression of me, sonny, so I'm making amends. I'm Benjamin Tinsdale. Old Ben, everyone calls me, because I've lived more years than most ten people."

Fargo scoured the street. "Where's the saloon?"

"There isn't one."

In all his wide-flung travels Fargo had never heard tell of a town that size without a watering hole. "The people here aren't Quakers, are they?"

Old Ben cackled. "Land sakes, no! I wish we did have a whiskey mill. I'd spend every waking minute there." He jabbed his bone-handled knife at an establishment across the street. "The closest we have is the Wolfrik Billiard Parlor. It ain't much, but they serve some right tasty foreign ale."

"How about whiskey?" Fargo asked, heading toward it. Several men were at the front window watching him.

"Afraid not," Old Ben said. "Hard liquor ain't allowed in Wolfrik. Sort of a town rule, you might say."

Fargo stopped in the center of the street. "How can that be? Don't tell me there's a temperance league here." The temperance movement had never been very popular west of the Mississippi, in large part because anyone foolhardy enough to try and shut down a saloon or tavern in a rowdy mining camp or a rough-and-tumble frontier town was likely to be shot for their efforts.

Old Ben cackled some more. I like you, sonny. You have a knack for tickling my funny bone. But no, we're not temperance boosters. Not by choice, anyhow."

"Are there any other rules I should know about?" Fargo asked, continuing on.

"A few." Ben recited them. "No spitting on the boardwalks, no cussing in public, no disrespect can be shown to the lady-folks, every able-bodied man is automatically a member of the fire brigade, no one is to be out and about after ten at night . . ."

Fargo stopped again. "Are you joshing me? Wolfrik has a curfew?" It was unheard of, and in his estimation as pointless as the ban on hard liquor.

"That's not all," Old Ben said. "Buildings must always be freshly painted, no one is allowed to have weeds in their yards, and all the businesses have to close on Sundays." Ben scratched his bushy beard, pondering. "Oh, I almost forgot. No one is allowed to go more than twenty miles from town in any direction."

"What kind of rule is that?"

"For safety's sake, sonny," Old Ben said. "There have been a few run-ins with the Flatheads of late. About two months ago a fella doing some prospecting was mutilated and scalped."

To the best of Fargo's knowledge the Flatheads were a friendly tribe. He mentioned as much. "Why are they acting up all of a sudden?"

"Your guess is as good as mine." Something in Old Ben's eyes and his tone suggested he knew more than he admitted.

Fargo almost regretted agreeing to have supper with the Jeeters. The more he learned about Wolfrik, the less he wanted to stick around. Squaring his shoulders he ambled into the billiard hall. The three men were involved in a game. Against the left wall was a bar and behind it were bottles of ale and beer arranged in separate rows.

A man with a handlebar mustache was wiping a mirror with a clean rag and merrily humming to himself. On hearing the jingle of Fargo's spurs, he turned. "Old Ben! Haven't seen you in a few days. And I see you've brought a friend along. What will it be, gents?"

"I'll take the usual, Tom," Ben said, placing the block of wood and his knife on the bar. "Unless by some miracle you've got some Scotch in stock?"

Tom chuckled. Unlike the majority of Wolfrik's citizens he

appeared to be perpetually happy. "You know better. If I smuggled any into town I'd be in more trouble than you can shake a stick at." He selected a particular bottle. "Here's that ale you like."

The label, Fargo observed, had a lot of writing in a foreign language. At a guess he pegged it as Transian. "I'll have the same," he requested.

"Another Trinken Ale coming up." Tom opened their bottles. "I sell more of these than all the other brands combined."

"It's that good?" Fargo said.

"It's that high in alcohol," Tom said, grinning. "Twice what most of the others have. Tastes like horse piss but it'll get you drunk after fifteen or twenty bottles."

"Or thirty," Old Ben amended, gluing his lips to his and greedily gulping.

Fargo tried a sip. As ale went it wasn't bad but he preferred genuine coffin varnish to a weak imitation. He tilted the bottle a second time and happened to glance at the mirror. The three billiard players were converging on him with less than friendly expressions. All three were young, in their late teens or early twenties, and wore the same style of store-bought clothes as everyone else.

Tom lost his sunny disposition in a hurry. "Billy!" he addressed the shortest of the trio. "What can I get you? Another drink?"

"We want a few words with the stranger," Billy responded, a sneer of contempt creasing his ferret face. "Consider us the welcoming committee."

Fargo had met their kind before. They were the town toughs, simpletons who saw themselves as the cocks of the walk and made it a point to harass newcomers and anyone else they didn't cotton to.

Old Ben shifted. "Leave him be, youngster. He ain't done you any harm. All he wants is a drink and he'll be on his way."

"I'm not leaving until tomorrow," Fargo corrected him, and almost laughed when Old Ben, Tom, and the young tough, all said, *"What?"* simultaneously. Not that it was any of their concern, but he revealed, "I'm taking a room at the hotel for the night." He wanted to see how they would react.

"The devil you say! " Old Ben declared. "You don't want to stay there. They overcharge for the rooms, and the beds are so soft you can drown in 'em."

Billy's beady eyes narrowed and he stared across the street at the millinery. "Your hankering to stay over wouldn't have anything to do with the Widow Jeeter, would it, mister?"

"What if it does?" Fargo rejoined, gripping his bottle of ale by the neck.

"She's off limits to the likes of you," Billy bristled. "I've taken a shine to her my own self."

"She already has a child," Fargo said as innocently as could be. "What does she need with another?"

It took several seconds for the insult to sink in. When it did, Billy snarled like a riled badger and hiked the cue over his head. "Think you're smart, don't you, bastard? Well, my pards and me will show you."

"Is that a fact?" Fargo said, and smashed the bottle over the tough's head. The bottle shattered and Billy oozed to the floor like so much melted wax. His companions gaped, stupefied by the turn of events, as did Tom behind the bar.

Old Ben tittered merrily, smacking his thigh in glee. "Lordy, that was a sight worth seein'! Serves the whippersnapper right!"

Fargo was waiting to see what the other two would do. One was working his mouth like a fish out of water. The other, a lanky character with a beaked nose, appeared to be the more intelligent of the pair and found his voice first.

"You hit him!"

"I'll hit you, too, if you don't go away and quit pestering me," Fargo stated. He was in no mood to tolerate their nonsense.

"Don't get your dander up," Beak-Nose bleated. "We're going." The pair bent and hoisted Billy off the floor. Supporting him, they moved to the doorway. Beak-Nose had to get in a parting comment. "Don't think this is the end of it, mister.

You'll hear from us again. You're just lucky I don't have a gun or I'd blow out your wick right here and now." Out they hustled, in a huff.

Fargo was glad they weren't wearing six-shooters. They were idiots, but he'd rather not gun them down if he didn't have to. As he turned to ask for another ale, it occurred to him that none of the men he had met so far went around heeled. Seaver, Barstow, Old Ben, the three toughs, not one wore a revolver. He asked Old Ben why.

"It's another of those silly rules. All our hardware is kept in a back room at the hotel. Mr. Fetterman has a key, but he's not allowed to pass out the guns unless we're under attack by hostiles. Duke Wolfrik's orders."

Fargo digested the revelation. "Are you saying all your pistols and rifles were confiscated?" He couldn't believe what he was hearing. Next to stealing another man's horse, the surest way for a man to become worm food was to take another's gun. Westerners took their right to bear arms seriously, a trait many Easterners and most foreigners couldn't comprehend. But then, they didn't have to worry about vicious outlaws, bloodthirsty hostiles, or ravening beasts on a daily basis.

It was Tom who answered, "The duke thinks firearms aren't necessary so long as we're under his protection."

"Damned decent of him," Fargo said dryly.

"Don't hold it against him, mister. We all agreed to his terms before we ever moved here," Tom said. "They were in the contract we signed."

Fargo looked at Old Ben, who scowled and nodded.

"Personally, I don't mind so much," Tom went on. "I never wore a gun anyway, so what's the difference? When I answered the advertisement in the newspaper back in St. Louis I was skeptical, sure. But then I met Duke Wolfrik. He has a way about him that inspires confidence. And when he confirmed he would set me up in business at his own expense, how could I refuse?"

Too much was being thrown at Fargo too fast. "Hold on. What advertisement are you talking about?"

"The one the duke put in all the papers," Tom clarified. "Let me show you. I clipped it out and saved it." Going to the end of the bar, he opened a drawer and ruffled through a stack of papers. "Ah. Here we go."

The duke had spared no expense. The ad took up half a page. Fargo read the following:

THE CHANCE OF A LIFETIME

Attention. All those with brave hearts and a spirit of adventure. Do you yearn for a better life? A secure future? Then I, Duke Otto Wolfrik, am the person you must come see. Join me in my great enterprise.

A sketch of the duke was included. It depicted him in a military uniform adorned with dozens of medals. In the crook of his left arm was a helmet topped by a long spike. Broad across the chest, he held himself ramrod straight as if at attention. Deep, brooding eyes dominated an undeniably handsome face crowned by a bald pate.

I have founded a new town on the frontier. A town that needs men and women with certain valuable skills if it is to prosper. Below is a list. If you are picked, I will pay all the costs you entail in relocating and will set you up in business at my own expense. If interested, be at the Heritage Hotel this Saturday at ten A.M. All questions will be answered to your complete satisfaction.

Sincerely,
Duke Otto Wolfrik

The list, Fargo saw, was long. It included a blacksmith, a hotel operator, a barber, and many more. "There's no mention of contracts."

"He told us about them at the meeting," Tom said. "The duke insisted everyone sign one so there wouldn't be any misunderstandings later. All they say, basically, is that so long as we live in his town we have to abide by his rules."

"He's added more of them as time goes by," Old Ben said. "Pretty soon we'll need a written list to keep track of 'em."

Just when Fargo thought he had heard it all. He ordered another ale and for the next quarter of an hour plied the two men with questions. He learned the current population of Wolfrik stood at thirty-three, including women and children. Originally, the duke had brought along dozens of workers to erect the buildings, but they left after the job was done. Supply trains from the States arrived once a month, at which time mail was handed out and collected. Fargo also learned Wolfrik lived in a mansion five miles north of town.

"We don't see him much," Old Ben related. "He comes in for grub and such every now and then, and goes to church when he's in the mood."

Fargo had seen the church when he rode in, at the far end of the street. It boasted a slender steeple and a bronze bell that glistened like molten fire.

"The duke is too busy to spend all his time in town," Tom defended the founder. "He's got big plans he's trying to carry out. He aims to carve out his very own empire. He told me so himself."

"An empire?" Fargo asked, and downed the last of his ale.

"A cattle empire. The duke thinks the market will grow to ten times what it is now, in just a few years. By then he'll have thousands of cattle ready to ship to market."

"And his very own town to ship them from," Fargo said.

"You make it sound like a bad thing," Tom replied. "The duke is planning ahead, is all. He's a smart man, the smartest I ever met. And thanks to him, twenty years from now, when I'm ready for a rocking chair, I'll have enough socked away to enjoy my waning days in comfort."

Fargo stretched to relieve a kink in his back. According to a clock on the wall he had forty-five minutes to kill before he was due at the Jeeter place. "Thanks for the drink," he said. Slapping down a coin in payment, he ambled outside. Over by the stable three men were climbing on mounts. Billy and his

21

partners were preparing to ride out. They glared as they went by, Billy a study in pure spite.

The Ovaro was dozing. Fargo led it to the stable and forked over the dollar and a half the stableman required for a night's stay. He paid extra to have the stallion fed oats instead of hay. Throwing his saddlebags over his right shoulder and his bedroll over his left, he yanked the Henry rifle from its saddle scabbard and ambled up the street to the hotel.

Old Ben was back in his chair, whittling away. "Did you see those three no-accounts fly out of town a while ago?"

Fargo nodded and strode to the door.

"They're up to no good, I'll warrant. If I were you I'd forget about staying over and sleep out under the stars. Healthier that way."

"They don't worry me," Fargo said.

"It's not them, it's the duke. He doesn't take kindly to troublemakers."

"Then he should kick those three out of Wolfrik," Fargo said, and entered an elegantly furnished lobby. At the front desk a nattily dressed man was scribbling on a sheet of paper. He was so engrossed in his work, he jumped when Fargo thumped the saddlebags down and announced, "I need a room for the night."

"You do?" The man smiled and shoved the register toward him. "I mean, of course you do. Welcome. You took me by surprise. We don't get visitors all that frequently. I'm Milo Fetterman, the proprietor."

"Makes me wonder how you stay afloat," Fargo said, accepting a quill pen Fetterman offered. "The duke must help out."

"You know about him?" Fetterman asked. "Yes, he does. He's subsidizing the hotel until it's financially solvent. He predicts that in less than a year we'll be crammed full every night." Fetterman selected a key from a row of pegs. "Here you go. Number Seven. Down the hall to your right."

The room was as elegantly furnished as the lobby. A canopy bed, a mahogany chest of drawers, and wood paneling were proof Duke Wolfrik never did anything halfway. Fargo tossed his bedroll and saddlebags onto the bed, propped his Henry in a corner, and examined himself in an oval mirror above the chest of drawers. He was caked with dust, and his beard was in bad need of a trim.

Fargo took a straight razor from his saddlebags. A crystal water basin had been provided but no water. Opening the door, he bellowed for Fetterman, who came dashing down the hall, gushing with enthusiasm.

"Yes, sir! What do you require? How may I be of service?"

Fargo thrust the basin at him. "Some warm water would be nice."

"If you don't mind my asking, would the gentlemen prefer a hot bath? We have tubs in the back. I can have one filled in, say, half an hour. And we have genuine imported soap, all the way from Kroshno, the capital of Transia. When you're done I guarantee you'll smell like a bouquet of roses."

"Just fill this and bring it right back."

Fetterman didn't know when to leave well enough alone. "How about a bar of soap anyway? And scented oil from Paris, France, for your hair? Compliments of the Hotel Wolfrik, of course."

"No."

"We also have Cuban cigars, the finest snuff money can buy, and a newspaper from Denver. Whatever you want, sir. Your every wish is my command."

Fargo had a thought. "If you really want to please me, rustle up a bottle of whiskey. I'll praise this place to high heaven everywhere I go."

"Will you, really?" Fetterman squealed. Clapping his hands, he darted off giggling to himself.

One thing was for sure, Fargo mused as he closed the door; the town of Wolfrik had more lunatics than most insane asylums. He spent the next several minutes sharpening the straight razor. At a tiny rap he opened the door again and beheld the glorious vision of a full bottle of whiskey perched on a sterling-silver tray, along with a gleaming crystal glass.

"One whiskey as requested," Fetterman proudly declared.

Not only was it redeye, but it was the best redeye money could buy. Fargo held the bottle aloft and whistled in appreciation. "I thought hard liquor was off limits in Wolfrik."

"Generally speaking, yes," Fetterman said. "But all the best hotels on the Continent serve liquor and the duke doesn't want his hotel to be inferior to theirs." He lowered his voice and looked over a shoulder as if to confirm they were alone. "No one else in town knows it, but just off the kitchen is a cabinet crammed with everything from bourbon to brandy. It's always kept locked to discourage theft, and I'm the only person the duke has entrusted with the key." He patted a pocket.

Opening the bottle, Fargo took several long swallows. A familiar burning wetness flowed down his throat, spreading welcome warmth throughout his belly. Smacking his lips, he remarked, "Next thing I know, you'll be telling me you can hook me up with a fallen dove for the night."

"A dove?" Comprehension dawned and Fetterman blushed. "Oh. You mean a female. I'm afraid that's beyond even my ability. The duke doesn't permit loose women to reside in Wolfrik. It's—"

"I know, I know," Fargo interrupted. "It's against the rules."

"You can't blame him." Fetterman was another of the duke's defenders. "Look at places like Denver and New Orleans. At night a man can't hardly walk the streets without being accosted by brash young females in skimpy attire."

"I know," Fargo said fondly. On his last visit to the former he had spent three energetic days and nights with one.

"Give me another five minutes and I'll have your water," Fetterman said. He started to go. "Would you care for a meal? We have fresh eggs and milk and a slab of beef that was delivered by the duke's men just yesterday."

"I'm eating elsewhere."

"How can that be? Wolfrik doesn't have a restaurant yet. The duke says it can wait until more people move in. Where can you possibly go?"

The man had overstepped himself. "You're from back East," Fargo said. It was a statement, not a query.

"Connecticut. Why?"

Slashing the air with the razor, Fargo answered, "Out here when a man sticks his nose where it doesn't belong, it gets chopped off."

Fetterman's Adam's apple bobbed. "My apologies, sir. I keep forgetting how sensitive frontiersmen are. About six weeks ago a buffalo hunter stopped for the night. A rather odoriferous fellow. When I politely mentioned he was rather ripe, he touched the muzzle of his buffalo gun to my nose and told me he could solve the problem right quick, as he phrased it." Fetterman sighed. "No offense, but sometimes I can't help thinking I've been thrown among barbarians."

"You have," Fargo said, closing the door. In his saddlebags was a spare set of buckskins, and after stripping, he unrolled them and donned the pants. He also wiped the dust and grime from his boots and cleaned dirt from his spurs. When the hot water arrived he trimmed his beard and the hair around his ears, washed his face and chest, and finished dressing.

Fargo knew he might be going to a lot of bother for nothing. Mary Jeeter was attractive, yes, but she had given no hints whatsoever that anything other than simple gratitude had sparked her invitation. He adjusted his red bandanna, put on his hat and gunbelt, and was ready.

Fetterman wasn't in the lobby. About to go out, Fargo noticed a vase containing yellow and blue flowers. He helped himself to a handful.

Old Ben had gone. The sun hovered on the far horizon, about to relinquish the sky to the stars. Fargo saw no sign of Wolfrik's thirty-three citizens even though it wasn't anywhere near curfew. Either they were all eating supper or word had spread and they were staying indoors to avoid him.

Fargo had to knock three times before he heard footsteps.

Mary Jeeter was positively breathtaking. She had done up her hair and now wore a tight green dress that clung to her shapely contours like a second skin. Beckoning, she flashed teeth as white as pearls.

"Come in. Please. We've been looking forward to this."

So had he, Fargo reflected. In more ways than one.

3

Tantalizing musky perfume wreathed Skye Fargo as he was ushered through the millinery shop into a modest sitting room. On the opposite wall hung a huge painting of a stern gray-haired man in seafaring garb.

"My grandfather," Mary said when she noticed Fargo staring at it. "He sailed for thirty years as a captain on a whaling vessel out of Nantucket and retired to a cottage overlooking the bay. As a girl I spent hours listening to his stories."

"What about your father?" Fargo asked making small talk.

"He was a greengrocer. Hated the sea and wouldn't set foot on a ship if his life depended on it." Mary indicated a chair. "Have a seat, please. Supper will be a few minutes yet. We can get better acquainted."

Fargo would have liked nothing better. Soft lantern light splashed over her golden tresses and exquisite features, heightening her beauty and adding to her sensual allure. Taking off his hat, he hung it on a peg and made himself comfortable.

"Jenny will be down in a moment. She's always late, that girl." Mary sank onto a settee. The hem of her dress started to hike toward her knees but she primly smoothed it out and folded her hands in her lap

Fargo didn't blame her for being cautious. They barely knew each other, and she had her welfare and her child to think of. To say nothing of her reputation. Single women were considered fair game by every rogue and roughneck in britches. They had to forever be on their guard against being taken advantage of. "Nice house you have," he politely commented.

"Thank you. Another nineteen years of paying off Duke Wolfrik, and the place will be mine, free and clear." Mary didn't sound particularly happy about it.

"What's he like?" Fargo fished for information.

Mary's face clouded, but she forced a smile to disguise her feelings. "I'm grateful to him. He gave Jenny and me a chance at a new life. I wanted to get away from Missouri, wanted to start over. I couldn't have done it without him."

For a widow with a child to take such a bold step and move to the frontier was highly uncommon, and Fargo complimented her. "You're very courageous."

"Oh, courage had nothing to do with it," Mary said. "I wanted to escape the memories. You see, it was three years ago this month that my husband, Edward, perished. We owned a combination feed store and millinery. One day when he was delivering feed to a local farmer the team spooked and the wagon overturned, crushing him."

"I'm sorry."

"I cried for weeks on end." Deep sorrow etched Mary's face. "The doctor tried to console me by saying Ed must have died instantly. As if it mattered. I'd lost the man I loved. I also lost our store because I couldn't keep the payments up on my own. Jenny and I were living in a cramped apartment and I was barely making ends meet when I saw the duke's advertisement in a local newspaper."

"Any regrets about coming here?" Fargo asked,

"Not a one," Mary answered, but it was as plain as her cherry-red lips she wasn't telling the truth.

Just then Jenny breezed into the sitting room, Samson tagging at her heels. "Mr. Fargo!" She came over and grasped his hand. "I wanted to thank you again for saving my dog. I was scared something awful had happened."

Fargo remembered Old Ben saying the girl would be better off if the mongrel never came back. "He runs off a lot, does he?"

"No, not at all." Jenny knelt and affectionately hugged her dog. "This was the first time. We had been playing out in the back yard. It's all fenced in and he's never gotten away before so I came in for a drink of water. When I went back out he was gone."

"How did he get out?"

"I wish I knew. There aren't any holes in the fence. And he didn't dig his way out." She kissed Samson and he licked her neck. "He just up and vanished."

Fargo was watching the mother and saw Mary Jeeter look away, deeply troubled. "Does the back fence have a gate?"

"No." Mary fidgeted, uncomfortable with the topic. "So it couldn't have been left open, if that's what you're thinking."

Fargo reached down to pat Samson and abruptly realized something he should have realized sooner. Ordinarily, frontier towns crawled with dogs and cats, with loose chickens and pigs and whatnot. But Samson was the only animal he'd seen the entire time he had been in Wolfrik, other than a few horses. "Do many people in town own pets?"

"I'm the only one," Jenny said. "The duke doesn't like it much, but he told my ma it's okay so long as I don't let Samson run around loose."

Fargo arched an eyebrow at Mary. "All these people and she has the only dog?"

"There's a rule against pets. Duke Wolfrik doesn't like them. He says dogs and cats soil our streets and make nuisances of themselves."

"But he made an exception in your case?"

"Sort of," Mary said. "Jenny has had Samson for over five years. They're inseparable, and I couldn't bear to leave him behind when we left Missouri. So I brought him along even though I shouldn't have."

Jenny giggled. "The duke sure was mad at first. But then he took a shine to ma and told us it was all right."

"Jennifer!" Mary declared. "That's not true."

"Everyone says so," Jenny held her ground. "I heard Mrs. McGillicutty and Mrs. Keating talking a while back. They said the duke is right fond of you. Mrs. Keating says if you had any sense you'd haul him to the altar."

"She did, did she?" Mary's full cheeks flushed with color. "You should know better than to believe the town gossip."

For Fargo's benefit Jenny mentioned, "Mrs. Keating probably said that because the duke comes here a lot. He's always bringing ma flowers and such."

"That's enough about me," her mother declared. "Why don't you go set the table? I'll be along in a minute."

Unfazed, Jenny skipped out, whistling to herself, and Samson pranced at her side, a contented shaggy shadow.

Mary Jeeter rose. "Girls her age are very impressionable. She's my daughter and I adore her dearly, but you have to take everything she says with a grain of salt."

"I hope the duke won't be upset when he finds out I came for supper," Fargo remarked. Not that he cared how the duke felt. "I wouldn't want to get you into trouble."

"I'm a grown woman and can have anyone over I like," Mary said defensively. "Duke Wolfrik doesn't own me. He has no right to tell me who I can and can't see, despite what he might think." She had grown so angry her fists were clenched.

"Has he been bothering you?"

Mary wheeled. "I'd rather not discuss it. If you'll excuse me, I'll see to our meal. It shouldn't be long."

Fargo had a lot to mull over while he waited, He'd never met Duke Otto Wolfrik but it was safe to say he didn't like the man. The impression he had was that Wolfrik liked to run roughshod over others, and he was surprised the townspeople stood for it. By and large frontier folk didn't like being told how they should live, a sentiment he shared.

A low *woof* sounded from the doorway. Samson was back. Fargo extended a hand and the dog padded over and licked his fingers. He thought about what Jenny had said. Plainly, Samson hadn't run off as everyone claimed. Someone had taken the dog and dumped it deep in the woods. It was a sheer fluke he had found the four-legged rascal before Samson died of starvation or thirst. But who in the world would do such a thing? Who could be so cruel to a girl and her pet?

"There you are!" Jenny skipped into the room and claimed her hairy friend. "Ma says it's time to eat."

A narrow hall brought them to a small but serviceable kitchen complete with a stove and a square table covered by a clean white cloth. Silverware already graced it, as did several candles in bronze holders. Stew was simmering in a giant pot and a heaping bowl of fresh vegetables had been set out.

"It isn't much," Mary apologized. "I don't bother with fancy meals often because it's just Jenny and me. If I'd had more notice, I'd have rustled up some steak and baked you a pie." She paused. "They were Ed's favorites."

About to sit down, Fargo hesitated when they both gazed apprehensively at his Colt. "Is something wrong?"

"Guns makes us nervous," Mary said. "My Ed never wore one, and I see no reason why you need to have yours on." She grinned self-consciously. "We didn't invite you here to assault you."

Fargo rarely took the Colt off. It was as much a part of him as his arms or his legs. The first thing every morning he strapped it on, and it was the last article he removed every night. On the few occasions he had traveled east of the Mississippi or been in towns where firearms were prohibited, he usually tucked the Colt under his shirt so it was out of sight but within quick reach.

"Please," Mary requested.

Against his better judgement Fargo unbuckled his gunbelt and hung it over the back of the chair. The right thing to do was honor her request. It was silly to balk when he was in no immediate danger.

"Thank you." Mary stepped to the stove. "Have a seat. There's no need to stand on formality." She opened a cabinet. "What would you like to drink? We have water, milk, or coffee."

"Coffee," Fargo said, and settled down to an enjoyable hour of delicious food and friendly conversation. Mary and Jenny did most of the talking, rambling on about how pleasant their life in Missouri had been and how tough it was to pull up stakes and move to Wolfrik. Eventually the topic turned to Ed Jeeter, and what a wonderful husband and father he had been.

Fargo mainly listened, nodding now and then and injecting a short comment or two.

The Jeeters had been like most couples in Jefferson City, Missouri. They were God-fearing, law-abiding, hard-working sorts who believed a rosy future was theirs for the asking. They'd borrowed heavily for the capital to start their business. After Ed died, Mary tried her best to stay afloat. But many of the feed store customers didn't much like the idea of doing business with a woman, or else their wives didn't like it. She'd lost practically everything except the clothes on their backs and a few simple possessions.

"I was so thrilled when I met Duke Wolfrik and he promised to help us out," Mary revealed. "He seemed like such a perfect gentleman."

"And now?" Fargo goaded.

"Now my ma doesn't like him much," Jenny said, her mouth crammed with bread and butter. "One time he came over and wanted to stay real late, but she wouldn't let him so they had an argument."

"No more, Jennifer! " Mary said severely. "How many times must I repeat myself? There are some things a lady doesn't discuss. Ever."

"If you don't want to stay in Wolfrik why don't you go back to the States?" Fargo suggested.

Mary's slender shoulders sagged. "I'm afraid that's not possible. I signed a contract like everyone else, and the duke has made it plain he intends to hold me to it."

"Then just up and leave."

"I've considered it. Believe me. But the Blues watch all the trails. Trying to sneak off with the supply wagons wouldn't be wise, either, because the Blues always check the wagons before they pull out,"

"Who are these Blues everyone keeps talking about?"

"Duke Wolfrik's Imperial Guard. Soldiers who are fiercely loyal to him and him alone. Men from the Old Country, descended from those who have been guarding the Wolfrik line for generations. We call them Blues because they wear blue uniforms."

"They're not very nice," Jenny threw in. "They don't let anyone talk back to them or say bad things about the duke."

"I can take you of out here tomorrow if you'd like," Fargo proposed. Anyone who tried to stop them would regret it. "Pack whatever you need. We'll ride out at dawn."

Mary bestowed a peculiar look on him, a look of gratitude and something else, something difficult to pin down. "I'm grateful for the offer, but I don't own any horses. We traveled here on the supply wagons."

Fargo was willing to help them out financially if need be. "We'll buy mounts. A horse for you and a pony for your daughter."

"Mr. Timmons, the stable owner, isn't allowed to sell horses to anyone who lives in Wolfrik without the duke's permission," Mary punctured his plan.

Fargo was amazed. Was Wolfrik a town or a prison? "And the people here let him get away with that?"

"Most like it here," Mary said, "They have no hankering to live anywhere else so they accept whatever the duke says."

Fargo had a dozen questions he wanted to ask, but he was distracted by the ripe contours of her body when she rose to refill his cup. Her red lips and the swell of her luscious breasts incited images better left alone. She turned to retrieve the coffeepot, the dress molding to her long thighs, and below his belt he stirred.

"Mr. Fargo?"

Fargo had momentarily forgotten about the girl. "What?" he absently replied.

"I hope you can find a way to help us. My ma isn't happy here. She's told me time and again she'd like to leave but she doesn't know how. After what happened to Samson I don't

33

want to stay, either. I love him. If I lost him again I don't know what I'd do."

"I'll see that both of you get back to the States safely," Fargo vowed. Although how he could accomplish it without mounts remained to be seen.

A sudden pounding from the front of the house stiffened the mother and her daughter in fear. "Someone is at the door!" Mary exclaimed. "Wait here and be quiet." She bolted down the hall.

Jenny leaned across the table and whispered, "I hope it's not who I think it is, Mr. Fargo. Maybe you should hide in the pantry."

Fargo did the next best thing. Rising, he strapped on his gunbelt and adjusted it at the height he was accustomed to. Loosening the Colt in its holster, he rotated as heavy footfalls approached.

A figure filled the doorway, a squat, powerful man wearing a neatly pressed blue uniform, polished black boots, and a metal helmet with a spike on the crown. A Blue. Both the uniform and helmet were identical to those in the sketch of the duke. The man took one look and jabbed a thick forefinger. "You! Stranger! You are to come with me this instant." His English was thickly laced with an accent.

"And if I don't?" Fargo said, deliberately placing his hand on the Colt.

"I will yell for the squad of Guardsmen waiting outside and we will drag you out of here against your will." The man put his brawny hands on his hips. "It's in your own interests to go along quietly."

Mary's fright was transparent. "Maybe you should do as Sergeant Dieter says," she recommended.

"No one asked your opinion, Mrs. Jeeter," Dieter declared. "And be advised the duke does not appreciate your shameful behavior. Inviting this man into your home is a serious breach of the rules."

Resentment replaced Mary's fear. "Now I can't have company when I want? Is that what you're telling me?"

Ignoring her, Sergeant Dieter moved toward Fargo. "Your weapon, sir, or we will take it from you."

"Over my dead body," Fargo said, and drew. His hand a blur, he slammed the six-gun against the sergeant's jaw.

Dieter was knocked backward. Shaking his head like a riled bull, he clawed for a revolver in a flap-covered holster on his left hip, but he had been dazed by the blow and he was much too slow.

Fargo smashed his Colt against the man's jaw a second time. The sergeant's knees buckled and he did a slow pirouette to the floor.

"You hit him!" Jenny marveled.

Mary was too astounded to say anything.

Fargo started toward her, then stopped when the front room resounded to the pounding tread of many boots. More Blues were on their way. He was prepared to confront them but Mary gripped him by the shirt and pushed him toward the rear door.

"For God's sake, leave! Out the back! Hurry!"

Fargo disliked turning tail. But if gunplay broke out, Mary and her daughter might take a stray slug. Reluctantly, he permitted her to hustle him across the kitchen and virtually shove him outside.

For a moment they locked eyes. Mary smiled warmly and squeezed his hand. "Thanks again for your kind offer. I wish we'd had more time to get acquainted. You're a fine man."

With that, the door was slammed in Fargo's face. He backpedaled as harsh voices flooded the kitchen, then he whirled and ran to the picket fence. Placing a hand on top, he vaulted over and flattened as the rear door was flung wide and a rectangle of light pierced the darkness.

Four men in blue uniforms filed out looking right and left, their large revolvers drawn and cocked.

Fargo held himself perfectly still. The Guardsmen were spreading out, checking the yard. One stalked directly toward him.

Out front more soldiers were yelling in Transian, and shadowy shapes moved along the street, seeking him.

The Blue walking in his direction abruptly veered to examine a row of rosebushes to the right. Fargo began to crawl off but stopped when a fifth Blue emerged. Words were exchanged and two of the men went back inside. Intent on the soldier poking into the roses, Fargo didn't notice another one coming from the front of the house along the outside of the picket fence until the telltale rustle of grass alerted him the Guardsman was only yards away.

Swiveling, Fargo pointed his Colt. The Blue was scanning the back yard and had no inkling he was there. Another few strides and the man would step on him. The next instant a shout from the kitchen spurred the men in the yard to hurry indoors. At the same time, the Blue next to the fence hastened toward the street.

Rising into a crouch, Fargo cat-footed to the front to see what was going on. A majority of the townsfolk had gathered for the same purpose and more were hurrying to the scene. Among them he recognized Old Ben, Tom from the billiard hall, Luke Barstow the blacksmith, Frank Seaver and his son Johnny, and even Fetterman, from the hotel.

Fargo's blood ran cold when he spotted the three toughs he had clashed with earlier standing near the front gate, Billy with his arms folded across his chest and a smug expression on his sadistic face.

Sergeant Dieter had recovered. Rubbing his jaw and glowering at everyone he passed, he stormed toward the horses. In his wake trailed four Blues with Mary and Jenny Jeeter in their grasp.

"Please! We don't want to go!" Mary protested.

"You have no choice, madam," Sergeant Dieter growled. "You must explain yourself to the duke." A Blue opened the gate for him and he stomped through to a waiting bay and snagged the reins.

Mary was forced to climb onto a sorrel. Jenny was flung

onto a dun. Mounted Blues nudged their horses on either side of the pair to prevent them from trying to escape.

As the sergeant forked leather the onlookers edged closer. A man Fargo didn't know made bold to call out, "Hold on there! Where are you taking Mary and her daughter?"

Dieter sat the saddle as if he were about to pass in review on a parade ground. "It is none of your affair, Mr. Richter. You—all of you—disperse and go on with whatever you were doing!"

"Like hell, sonny," Old Ben responded. "It ain't right to drag a lady off at this time of night. How do we know you're not up to no good?"

The implication elicited a sneer from Dieter. "How crude you Americans are. I am a soldier, Mr. Tinsdale. A professional. I do not trifle with women, nor do I harm them or hurt small children." He lifted his reins. "As for Mrs. Jeeter, Duke Wolfrik has requested her presence and I am to serve as her escort."

Old Ben wouldn't let it drop. "How do we know *he's* not up to no good?"

Sergeant Dieter swung his bay toward the crowd, bearing down on them so rapidly they scattered to keep from being trampled. At the last instant he reined up, the bay mere inches from Old Ben, who hadn't budged. "I will thank you, Mr. Tinsdale, not to insult the duke in my presence. Duke Wolfrik is an eminently honorable man. He would no more stoop to imposing himself on a woman than I would."

"He'd better not," Frank Seaver declared. "There are some things we just won't stand for and that's at the top of the list."

The Blues had lined up in pairs, each man as stiff-backed as a broomstick, their metal helmets glittering in the lanternlight. Sergeant Dieter raised an arm, then held it there when the blacksmith, Luke Barstow, bellowed, "Widow Jeeter better be brought back soon or we'll come looking for her. Be sure and tell the duke!"

Dieter raked the crowd with a look of contempt. "Rabble

and riffraff," he declared, and whipped his arm in a crescent. The Blues cantered northward, the column raising swirls of dust in its wake.

The townspeople were slow to disperse. Old Ben stepped onto the boardwalk and climbed onto an empty wooden crate in front of the general store. "How long?" he demanded. "How long are we going to let the duke get away with treatin' us like we're no-account?"

"Don't start, Ben," Fetterman said. "Just because you're unhappy with the status quo is no excuse to stir up trouble."

"Some of us don't have the low opinion of the duke you do," Tom from the billiard hall mentioned.

"You'll change your minds sooner or later," Old Ben said. "Once you get tired of licking the duke's shoes. Once you see him for the polecat he really is."

"Spare us," Fetterman said, heading for the hotel. "We've heard it all before and it's as tiresome now as it was then."

Presently only the old-timer, Frank Seaver, and Luke Barstow were left. "You'll never get them to agree," the blacksmith said. "Not so long as the duke is careful not to provoke them too far."

Ben swore luridly. "He controls them. How they live. What they think. It's downright pitiful no one has the gumption to stand up to him."

"Brave words," Frank Seaver said, "but you don't have a wife and children to think of. You don't have as much to lose as most of us."

They launched into a heated dispute that Fargo didn't stick around to hear. He intended to go after the Jeeters. First, though, he glided to the rear of the house, hopped over the fence, and went in through the back door. He had to retrieve his hat, which he'd left hanging on a peg in the sitting room.

Fargo quick-stepped down the hall and into the sitting room. He was almost to the peg when a shadow flitted across the wall, warning him he wasn't alone. He spun but he didn't try for his Colt.

A pair of husky soldiers stood under the painting of Mary's grandfather, each with a leveled revolver. "Greetings, American," one said in English more heavily accented than Dieter's. "Our sergeant thought you would return, so he left us behind to welcome you. Be so kind not to move or we will shoot you dead."

4

Skye Fargo had blundered, not once but twice. His first mistake had been in not realizing two of the Blues were unaccounted for since Mary and Jenny had ridden off on their mounts. His second mistake had been in waltzing into the house with his guard down, right into a clever trap arranged by the wily Dieter.

The two Blues separated and came at him from opposite sides, their revolvers as steady as steel. Their weapons, Fargo saw, were Beaumont-Adams .44-caliber models manufactured by the Massachusetts Arms Company. Big and heavy, they weren't as highly regarded as guns put out by Colt, Remington, or Smith and Wesson. But they were every bit as deadly.

"Now then," said the soldier who knew English, "I want you to do exactly as I say. No tricks. No quick moves. Understand?"

"I savvy," Fargo said, taking their measure. Neither had cocked their revolver, a crucial mistake he might be able to exploit.

"Excellent. You will stand perfectly still while my friend relieves you of your gunbelt. Any attempt at trickery will be harshly dealt with."

Despite their uniforms they were amateurs. The second Blue holstered his sidearm and stepped directly between Fargo and the soldier covering him. The man reached for Fargo's belt buckle, in the process turning himself into a human shield.

Fargo seized the moment. He drove a knee up into the careless Blue's groin, and when the man started to double over, he pushed, shoving the second Blue into the first. Both went down. The soldier who had been covering him dropped the Beaumont-Adams. The other clutched himself and groaned.

Taking a step, Fargo unlimbered the Colt and brought it crashing down on top of the soldier he had kneed. He shifted to do the same to the first Blue, but the man shot up off the floor as if fired from a catapult and tackled him around the waist.

Fargo managed to swing once before he smacked onto his back, but he was off balance and his Colt glanced off the Blue's collarbone. He tried to land another blow, but the soldier gripped his wrist with one hand and his throat with the other and proceeded to throttle the life out of him.

"How dare you lay a hand on a member of Duke Wolfrik's Imperial Guard!" the Transian hissed. He was furious, his lips drawn back over his teeth as if he were a rabid wolf about to bite.

Fargo sought to breathe but couldn't. He heaved upward but was unable to dislodge his attacker. Levering a knee into the man's chest did no good, either. Only when he resorted to smashing his forehead into the soldier's face did he succeed. There was an audible *crunch,* and a damp, sticky sensation prickled his forehead.

The man's grip slackened.

Fargo hurled the Blue off and surged erect as moist blood trickled into his left eye. Blinking to clear it, he connected with a left cross as the soldier was rising.

The man staggered against the wall, wobbly but refusing to give in. He coiled to launch himself forward but stopped when Fargo pointed the Colt at his sternum. "Go ahead, American!" he spat. "Shoot me! I will gladly die in service to my duke! Slay me and be done with it."

Wondering what it was about Otto Wolfrik that inspired such loyalty, Fargo responded, "All I want is answers. For starters, why did he send for Mary Jeeter and her daughter?

"To question them about you. What else?" The soldier wiped the back of a hand across his ravaged nose. Blood was streaming down over his mouth, painting his chin scarlet.

"That's all?"

"That's enough. We received a report you were a trouble-maker, that you started a fight in the billiard hall."

"Let me guess," Fargo said. "Billy and his friends."

"Herr William Travers and his companions filed the complaint. Duke Wolfrik dispatched us to take you into custody until an inquest could be held."

Backing away, Fargo picked up the .44 the man had dropped and plucked the other .44 from the second guardsman's holster. "See to your friend and do something about your nose before you bleed to death." He sidled to the peg, reclaimed his hat, and sidestepped to the doorway.

"You're not going to shoot us?" the man asked in mild surprise.

"I'm no killer," Fargo replied. Pivoting, he dashed to the front door and checked if it was safe to go further. The street was deserted. He jogged to the gate, tossing the pair of Beaumont-Adams revolvers into the rosebushes as he went by. Turning right, he raced toward the hotel. Boisterous talk and laughter issued from the billiard hall, but he paid it no mind.

Fetterman was at the front desk. He looked up, his jaw muscles working in a wonderful imitation of someone attempting to swallow an apple whole. "You!" he blurted.

"Me," Fargo said, breezing toward his room.

"Hold on," Fetterman said. "You can't—that is—I mean—I was at Widow Jeeter's. I know the duke is looking for you and I don't care to antagonize him."

"Leave that to me."

Fargo's belongings were right where he had left them. He closed his saddlebags, rolled up his bedroll, and tucked them under an arm. Cradling the Henry, he opened the window, slipped out, then quietly shut it behind him. If more Blues came looking for him Fetterman would think he was still there.

Sticking to shadows, Fargo bent his steps toward the stable. Dieter's bunch had a five-minute lead, but he figured he could overtake them before they reached the duke's place if he hurried.

Fargo was abreast of the billiard parlor when more gruff laughter pealed. Glancing over, he saw half a dozen men inside, one of whom had his back to the window and was entertaining the others with a tale of some kind. The man shifted, and his face was cast in profile by the lantern light.

Anger boiled in Fargo. Setting the bedroll and his saddlebags on the boardwalk, he crossed the street.

Billy Travers had his back to the entrance. "Yes, sir, boys. No one does that to me and gets away with it. I had the duke convinced a regular hellion had stormed into town and would tear the place up unless he did something."

Some of the men chuckled. Tom was filling a glass with ale.

"I only wish I'd been able to wallop that bastard a few times," Billy bragged. "Hell, just once would do."

Fargo was through the doorway and beside the young tough in two long bounds. "Like this?" he said, and when Billy whirled, startled witless, he smashed the Henry's stock against the younger man's cheek. Once, then twice, and Billy crumpled like paper, his cheek split wide. When he came to rest two of his teeth were lying beside him.

"Anyone else?" Fargo challenged, spinning toward the others.

Billy's two pards were pale as sheets, while the rest of the townsmen were too dumfounded to think of lifting a finger against him.

"It wouldn't be healthy to follow me," Fargo warned, and backed out before they could come to their senses. Snatching up his bedroll and saddlebags on the fly, he sped to the stable, only to find the wide double doors closed and barred on the inside.

"Damn," Fargo said, and turned. Most stables had side doors and this one was no different. The latch squeaked as he pressed it, but no one challenged him as he roved along the center aisle to the stall containing the Ovaro. His bridle, saddle, and saddleblanket were draped nearby. Fargo brought the stallion out and within three minutes was ready to leave. He gave the cinch a last tug to tighten it to his satisfaction and stepped into the stirrups. As he made for the wide doors a shadow detached itself from a wall.

"You're leavin' awful late," the stableman, Timmons, remarked.

"Keep the stall for me," Fargo said. "I don't expect to be gone all that long." That was, if he made it back alive.

The stableman removed the long wooden bar and pushed on a door. "Better watch yourself. A band of Flatheads were spotted a ways west of here yesterday. Word has it they're out for fresh scalps."

"I'll keep my eyes skinned," Fargo said, applying his spurs. He bore right at the corner and rode between the stable and the church, then reined to the north once he was in the clear.

A sliver of crescent moon dominated star-filled heavens. Tall grass hemmed the road, waving and rippling in stiff wind.

Fargo brought the Ovaro to a gallop, every now and then rising in the stirrups to scan ahead for sign of the Blues. He was determined to do what he could to help Mary and Jenny. Not only to see them safely home but to help them go back East. Contract or not, the duke had no right to keep the Jeeters or anyone else in Wolfrik against their will. It might not be illegal, but it was certainly wrong. He would have Old Ben spread word around town, let it be known anyone who wanted to leave was welcome to do so. Seaver and others were bound to leap at the chance.

For over a mile and a half Fargo rode hellbent for leather without spotting Dieter's column. Then he glimpsed movement. He also spied glimmering lights miles off, in foothills bordering the plain. The duke's estate, he reckoned.

Soon riders appeared, filing northward. Fargo slowed, looking for the telltale gleam of moonlight on metal helmets and listening for the rattle of accouterments. But he saw none, heard none, and as he narrowed the distance he observed that the riders weren't riding in twos, as the Blues had been doing.

They were in a knot, and there were only five or six. Nowhere near as many as there should be.

Fargo wondered if Sergeant Dieter had ordered some of the Guardsmen to drop behind to discourage townsmen who might come after them. He dismissed it as unlikely. For one thing, backbone was scarce in Wolfrik. For another, if the riders were Blues, they should be in pairs, calvary fashion.

Yet if they weren't townsfolk and they weren't soldiers, who *were* they?

The obvious answer caused Fargo to slow even more. They had to be Indians. Flatheads, to be exact. The stableman had warned him a band was in the area and here they were, trailing the Blues. It didn't bode well.

Fargo couldn't recall a single previous instance where Flatheads had spilled white blood. They'd always been peaceful. For decades they had regularly visited trading posts to swap furs for trade goods, and not once in all that time had they caused trouble. The reverse was true. The tribe had gone out of its way to welcome white settlers, and had even sent delegations to St. Louis to learn more about white ways and receive instruction in white religion. So why were some now up in arms?

Flathead Lake was named after the tribe even though they no longer inhabited the region around it. They had been driven off long ago by the Blackfeet, who acquired guns and horses early on and pushed several neighboring tribes into the mountains, among them the Flatheads. Once they obtained firearms and mounts of their own they'd begun making frequent forays to their old haunts. Each summer bands came down to hunt buffalo and trade with the whites.

So it stood to reason the men in front of Fargo were members of just such a band, probably the same warriors who had mutilated and scalped the prospector Old Ben had mentioned. In another fifty yards they separated. Half went into the high grass on the right, the rest into the high grass to the left.

Fargo rose in his stirrups. Well beyond the war party were more riders. The dull glint of helmets identified them. The

Blues were completely unaware they were being stalked. Sergeant Dieter and his men would be picked off one by one, their guns rendered impotent by the darkness.

Fargo didn't care what happened to the Guardsmen, but he did care about Mary and Jenny. If a fight broke out they might be slain, and he couldn't allow that. Clucking to the pinto, he angled into the grass on the right.

The problem was to discourage the Flatheads without killing them. Fargo wasn't an Indian-hater. He didn't agree with the widely held belief that the only good Indian was a dead Indian. He had lived among different tribes at one time or another and learned to respect them for who they were. In his eyes they were no different than the whites. They were people, human beings, men and women with the same natures, the same basic yearnings, the same flaws.

The Flatheads must have a reason for going on the warpath. Until Fargo learned what it was he wouldn't sit in judgment. Instead, he would strive his utmost to avoid spilling blood.

Hunching over the saddle horn, Fargo looped in a wide circle that brought him up on three warriors moving in a single file parallel to the Guardsmen without the warriors noticing. The Flatheads were intent on the soldiers. They weren't expecting anyone to come up behind them.

Slowly, soundlessly, Fargo pulled the Henry from its saddle scabbard. He quietly worked the lever, feeding a cartridge into the chamber.

Oblivious to the peril they were in, the Blues trotted on toward the hills. Mary and Jenny were behind Sergeant Dieter, Mary with her lovely head bowed, Jenny with her chin jutting defiantly.

Fargo couldn't see the Flatheads who were on the other side of the road. Hoping they didn't attack before the trio in front of him, he kneed the stallion and began to close on the third warrior.

Suddenly the lead Flathead raised a bow, pulled an arrow

from a quiver on his back, and nocked the shaft to a sinew string.

Wedging the Henry to his shoulder, Fargo took a bead. He wasn't close enough to stop the man any other way. But as his finger curled around the trigger an unexpected development brought the column of Blues to a halt. The Flatheads stopped, too, and the warrior lowered the bow.

Jenny Jeeter had reined the dun around and was making a bid to get away. Her small arms and legs flapping, she goaded the animal down the line of soldiers.

"Jenny, no!" Mary cried.

The girl didn't get ten yards. A Guardsman grabbed hold of the dun's bridle, bringing it to a halt. Incensed, Jenny lashed at his arm with her reins, yelling, "Let go of him! Let go! Do you hear me!" But she was too small for her blows to have any effect. The man grinned, which made Jenny madder still.

Sergeant Dieter rode up next to her horse. "That will be enough out of you, child," he said harshly. "This is the second time you have tried to run off. I won't tolerate a third attempt."

"I hate you!" Jenny declared. "You're a mean bully, just like the duke!"

"Have I harmed you or your mother?" Dieter retorted, and answered his own question. "No, not ever. Have I treated you improperly? Again, no. So why despise me so? I only do as I am ordered."

"We don't want to see Duke Otto," Jenny said. "Let us go so we can go back home where we belong."

Mary brought the sorrel down the row. "Don't try anything like that again," she cautioned her offspring. "You might have been hurt."

Jenny gestured. "Tell them! Make them leave us be!"

Fargo admired the child's grit. But more important at the moment were the warriors, who were puzzled by her attempt. Taking advantage, he slowly drew closer to the last one. Another twenty feet and he would be close enough to strike.

"I could talk to them until I was blue in the face and it

47

wouldn't do a lick of good," Mary was saying. "They don't give a hoot what we want."

"True enough," Sergeant Dieter said. "I am pledged to the service of the duke. Just as my father was, and his father before him. When a noble of the House of Wolfrik issues a command I am obligated to fulfill it or perish in the attempt."

"I've heard a rumor to that effect," Mary said, taking the dun's reins in hand. "Word is, you'd all die for him if you had to."

"It is no exaggeration," Dieter confirmed. "To be a Guardsman is an exceptional honor. We would gladly throw ourselves in front of a bullet or arrow to save Duke Wolfrik's life."

Fargo figured they might just get the chance. The foremost Flathead once again elevated his bow.

"I want to go home," Jenny forlornly reiterated. "Samson is all alone and must miss me." She gazed out over the sea of grass. "And I don't much like being out here so late at night. It's spooky."

Sergeant Dieter moved toward the head of the column. "We will be at the duke's soon, child. There you will be well taken care of. The maid will treat you to a plate of cookies and warm milk as she always does."

"I don't want cookies," Jenny argued, I want my dog."

The lead Flathead was taking deliberate aim. A tall warrior, he wore beaded buckskins and moccasins. As was customary, his dark hair hung in long braids. Paint streaked his face, and various symbols had been painted on his warhorse.

Fargo couldn't hold off any longer. Spurring the Ovaro, he let out with a fierce whoop and bore down on the last warrior. Startled, the Flathead shifted toward him, full into the barrel of the Henry, which Fargo swung, as if it were a club. The impact knocked the man off and sent him sprawling.

Without breaking the stallion's stride Fargo reined toward the second warrior. Once more the element of surprise worked in his favor. He struck the Flathead across the chest and sent him sprawling.

The tall warrior though, was another matter. He swiveled,

took in the situation at a glance, and as his second friend fell he loosed the shaft.

The barbed point clipped a whang on Fargo's buckskin shirt. Before the tall Flathead could snatch another arrow from his quiver, Fargo was on top of him. He swung the Henry, but the warrior ducked. Bringing the Ovaro to a halt, he reined around to try again.

The tall warrior was galloping eastward. He had swung onto the far side of his warhorse and only a forearm and an ankle were visible.

Over on the road a revolver banged. Then another.

Fargo glanced at the column and saw one of the Blues swaying in the saddle. A feathered shaft jutted from the soldier's chest. Another had been transfixed through the shoulder.

The Flatheads on the other side of the road had mistaken Fargo's whoop for a signal to attack. He heard Sergeant Dieter bellow in Transian. The column split, half swinging to the east, the other half to the west. With marked precision—evidence of countless hours spent drilling—they whipped out their Beaumont-Adams .44's. It dawned on him what they were about to do, and hauling on the Ovaro's reins, he sped to the northeast.

One of the Flatheads was still down, but the other had unsteadily risen and was trying to catch his animal.

A thunderous volley blistered the crisp air, Each of the Guardsmen fired twice, peppering the high grass on both sides.

The warrior who had just stood up was jolted by a slug that tore into his back between the shoulder blades and exited to the left of his sternum. He was dead when he hit the ground but he convulsed as if throwing a fit. His horse was also struck. Rearing, it whinnied stridently, its front hooves windmilling. Then it ran off, blowing noisily through its nostrils.

Fargo never liked to see a horse suffer, He started to rein the stallion toward it when the warhorse stumbled and dropped onto its front knees. Blowing froth, the animal keeled over, thrashed its legs a few seconds, and expired.

The Guardsmen were hastening northward, their revolvers at the ready, a ring of blue uniforms protecting Mary and Jenny Jeeter.

Fargo let them go. He couldn't get close now, not when they were ready to shoot anything that moved, He had to content himself with shadowing them, as the war party had been doing, only he stayed farther back in the grass. Presently, darkling foothills reared. The road wound up through ranks of stately pines to an estate worthy of royalty. An imposing mansion was the centerpiece, flanked by a stable and a long barracks. Additional outbuildings had been erected, mostly sheds and outhouses, along with a corral and a large log structure set off by itself.

Sergeant Dieter led his men to the foot of stone steps leading to a white portico. At his order the Blues dismounted. Dieter and four others escorted Mary and Jenny Jeeter to the front door. Others carried the two men who had been wounded to a small building near the barracks.

The sergeant gripped a large brass knocker and rapped. A gray-haired man in a black cutaway coat and striped trousers admitted them.

Fargo saw everything from the trees. He watched as more Blues emerged from the barracks to see what was going on. He also spied several sentries, posted at regular intervals around the perimeter. Sliding from his saddle, he wrapped the reins around a low tree limb, removed his spurs and placed them in a saddlebag, and crept to the right.

A woodshed was only a stone's throw from the pines. If Fargo could reach it he would be within sprinting distance of the barracks. From there he would be able to reach the mansion unseen.

The sentries were all interested in the new arrivals; no one was keeping an eye on the forest.

Easing onto his stomach, Fargo crawled toward the shed. He held the Henry in front of him and kept his chin low to the ground. Were the moon any brighter he would stand out like the proverbial sore thumb, but as it was, the woodshed's shadow concealed him adequately enough for him to snake up next to it and rise.

Gliding to the opposite corner Fargo surveyed the lawn. The long barracks were sixty feet away, and he would be exposed to the sentries most of the way across. But if he moved slowly and silently, avoiding their direct gaze, he might make it.

A long shot Fargo thought as he lowered himself. He held the Henry by the barrel and slid it along beside him leaving one hand free. Crabbing a couple of inches, he stopped and waited ten seconds, then pulled himself forward a couple more. It became a pattern.

At any moment Fargo expected to hear an outcry or the blast of a gun, but he went undetected. He was a third of the way to the barracks when a match flared to his left, bathing a pair of Guardsmen in its glow. He mimicked stone, waiting for them to move on, but they were talking and smoking, both leaning on their rifles, in no great hurry to get wherever they were going.

The front door opened. Out came Sergeant Dieter and the four Blues who had gone in with him. The sergeant made a beeline for the long barracks, the rest of the detail tiredly trudging along.

The two Guardsmen to Fargo's left slung their rifles over their shoulders and headed for the log structure.

Fargo crawled on. The wind grew stronger, rustling the trees. From the snowcapped peaks to the north wavered the lonesome wail of a wolf. To the west one of its kind answered. Moments later a mountain lion screeched, its cry eerily reminiscent of a woman in the throes of agony.

Judging by the noise coming from the barracks Fargo could tell Dieter and company weren't turning in. Maybe they were waiting to see if the duke intended for them to escort the Jeeters back to town. At any moment they might reappear. He had to go faster, had to reach the rear of the barracks before that occurred.

Taking a gamble, Fargo crawled on without stopping. He hadn't gone far when another scream rent the night. Only this one came from inside the mansion.

From the throat of Jenny Jeeter.

5

Skye Fargo couldn't help himself. He was up and running toward the mansion before the scream faded, flying full-out heedless of the risk. He knew the Blues would spot him, knew the smart thing to do was to continue to work his way to the mansion unseen. But Jenny and her mother needed him then and there.

Shouts rang out. Guardsmen hollered for him to stop. Sentries and others moved to intercept him. But no shots were fired thanks to Sergeant Dieter, who stepped from the stable and bawled commands in Transian, apparently telling the Guardsmen not to shoot, and to take him alive.

A burly Blue abruptly barred Fargo's path. Extending a hand palm-out, the soldier placed his other hand on the sidearm at his waist and barked in English, "In the name of the duke I order you to halt!"

Fargo did no such thing. Lowering his shoulders, he slammed into the Guardsman like a human battering ram, bowling the man over. Angry outcries followed but still none of the soldiers opened fire. If nothing else, Duke Wolfrik's Imperial Guard was a highly disciplined unit.

The fleetest of the Blues was only twenty feet away when Fargo reached the base of the steps and bounded up them three at a stride. At the top he didn't bother to knock. He flung the door inward and it crashed against the wall, the noise resounding down a long, wide hallway decorated with paintings and sculptures that Fargo barely noticed as he sprinted in search of the Jeeters.

The gray-haired servant in the black cutaway coat and

striped trousers stepped from a room just ahead and gaped in surprise.

The butler, Fargo figured, and stopped. "Where's Mary Jeeter and—" he began, then spied both mother and daughter in the room. Mary was holding Jenny protectively to her side, and Jenny's mouth was wide in horror.

Shoving the butler aside, Fargo darted across the threshold and leveled the Henry at the only other person there.

The sketch of Duke Otto Wolfrik had only hinted at his imposing presence. He stood six feet, three inches tall in polished knee-high black boots. Wide shoulders and a barrel chest tapered to a narrow waist girded by a broad black leather belt. His uniform was immaculate. Gold braid epaulettes, several rows of glittering medals, and gold trim at the collar and along the wide cuffs added luster. Flared knee-britches tucked into the tops of the boots. But the most striking feature was his face; broad, hawkish, with a hooked nose, a pointed chin, and a pair of penetrating green eyes crowned by a smooth bald pate that glistened as if he polished his head to the same sheen as his boots.

The duke stood next to a fireplace. Arrayed on the mantle were half a dozen large glass jars. In each lay coiled an enormous rattler. One of the jars had been ópened, and the duke now held its occupant by the back of the head.

"What the hell is going on?" Fargo demanded,

Mary and Jenny turned, relief washing over the mother, amazement over the girl. "Mr. Fargo!" Jenny exclaimed.

Duke Otto Wolfrik wasn't the least bit flustered. At complete ease, he smiled and regarded Fargo with intense curiosity. "So you are the gentleman I have been hearing so much about." he said in impeccable English.

The hall drummed to the beat of many boots. Another moment, and into the room spilled Sergeant Dieter and seven Blues. More filled the hallway. All had their weapons drawn except for the sergeant, who at sight of the duke immediately snapped to attention. The rest were quick to emulate his example.

Dieter addressed the duke in Transian, but Wolfrik held up a hand, silencing him. "In English, if you please, Sergeant. Have you forgotten my rule?"

"When in America do as Americans do and use their language as often as we can," Dieter recited. "My apologies, sir. For that, and for this intrusion. We were in fear for your life."

Duke Wolfrik gestured with the same hand that held the snake, which set the rattlesnake to whipping its body and rattling its tail. "I appreciate your concern. But you can leave."

"Sir?" Sergeant Dieter said uncertainly, glancing at Fargo.

"You are dismissed, Sergeant. Have the men stand down. I am in more danger from this helpless reptile"—Wolfrik gave the snake another shake—"than I am from our uninvited guest."

"As you wish, sir. But we will be right outside if you need us." Reluctantly, the sergeant and the others left, the glares they gave Fargo laced with the threat of violence if he dared harm the man they served.

"They're quite devoted, are they not?" Duke Wolfrik boasted, not without a touch of genuine affection.

"You must pay them well," Fargo commented. Training the Henry squarely on the duke's abdomen he moved nearer to Mary and Jenny.

Wolfrik made a sniffing noise. "I would construe that as an insult were it not for your abysmal ignorance. The Imperial Guard was created over three centuries ago. Becoming a member is considered the highest of honors a commoner can attain. They protect me out of a sense of duty, not for paltry money."

"How many are there?" Fargo inquired. It was always nice to know how many he was up against.

"Four hundred. The majority are still in Transia. Over two hundred alone, the largest contingent, are assigned to protect the king and queen."

"How many did you bring with you?" Fargo amended.

"Forty, not counting the good sergeant," The rattlesnake wriggled in Wolfrik's grasp, hissing and flicking its tongue, and he glanced down at it in amusement. "I almost forgot about you." He held the serpent toward Fargo. "These creatures are most magnificent, are they not? We have nothing like them in the Old Country, and they quite fascinate me." Wolfrik turned toward the mantle. "As you can see I've started a collection. They are abundant in the hills hereabout."

Fargo watched as the duke lowered the snake into the empty jar, tail first. The rattler automatically coiled, its eyes baleful pools of spite, as the duke casually withdrew his hand and lowered a wooden lid that had air holes in it so the snake wouldn't suffocate.

Wolfrik patted the jar and the snake rattled again. "I feed them mice and whatever else my men can catch." He glanced up. "Have you ever seen one of these creatures kill prey?"

Fargo nodded. Diamondbacks, timber rattlers, banded rattlers, sidewinders, pygmy rattlers, he had encountered them all.

"They are supremely efficient. One strike, and whatever they have bitten is done for." Wolfrik sounded as if he envied them. "They are consummate killers, these American vipers. I think when I go back to Transia I shall take some along and breed them in my native land."

"The people there won't mind?" Fargo asked.

"What they want is irrelevant," Duke Wolfrik said, clasping his hands behind his back. "Royal blood flows in my veins. My decisions are above censure." He stared at the Henry. "You can lower your weapon, if you please. I've demonstrated my intentions are peaceful."

Fargo looked at the Jeeters. "Are the two of you all right? I heard a scream."

"That was me," Jenny said, jutting her lower lip at their royal host. "He scared me half to death."

"But he didn't mean to," Mary said.

Duke Wolfrik hadn't taken his gaze off the rifle. "I would never deliberately scare a child." He nodded at the jar he had just replaced. "I was taking the snake out to show them and it nearly wriggled loose. Sweet Jennifer was afraid it would bite her." He bowed at the waist. "Kindly accept my humble apologies."

Mary smiled halfheartedly. "No real harm was done."

"Then all is forgiven?" Wolfrik said cheerfully.

Fargo lowered the Henry's muzzle so it was pointing at the floor, but he kept his finger on the trigger and his thumb on the hammer. "Forget the snake. Let's talk about dragging the Jeeters here against their will."

" 'Drag' is a rather harsh term, yes?" Duke Wolfrik said. "My Guardsmen requested Mary's presence, is all. Neither she nor her daughter were mistreated."

Fargo glanced at the mother, thinking she would tell the duke how she truly felt, but once again she hedged.

"We weren't given a choice, though," Mary said. "Your men tend to forget this is America. Things are done differently here."

"So I've noticed," Duke Wolfrik said wistfully. "In my country we adhere to the old ways. To a monarchy and a royal line of descent. Everyone knows their proper place, from the king down to the lowliest peasant. Our government and our society, are orderly. There is none of the chaos that distinguishes this untamed land."

"Our system of government is as good as yours," Mary said defensively.

Wolfrik dismissed the notion with a snort. "I beg to differ, dear lady. In Transia royalty is recognized as special and treated accordingly. To us, America's obsession with the rights of the rabble is pitiable. It's an earmark of political immaturity."

Fargo would be hard-pressed to come up with a subject that interested him less than politics. Touching Mary's arm, he said, "I'll take you back to town now if you want."

"Is that all right with you?" Mary asked the duke.

"Absolutely not. You've only just arrived." Wolfrik nodded at a plush sofa. "Make yourselves comfortable and I'll have refreshments brought." To the butler he said, "Bring the usual for Mrs. Jeeter, her daughter, and myself. As for Mr. Fargo, the famed frontiersman, I imagine he wants something a little stronger than jasmine tea or hot chocolate."

"Whiskey," Fargo said. "And how is it you know who I am?"

"You signed the register at my hotel, remember?" Duke Wolfrik mentioned as the butler departed. "And your name is not unknown to me. At Fort Leavenworth I had a most interesting discussion with a major about the U.S. Army in general, and army scouts in particular. You were mentioned in a most flattering light. He told me you are one of the best frontiersmen alive. The military has relied on your skills more times than he could remember."

"I've worked for them on occasion," Fargo allowed.

Mary was moving toward the sofa, her hand on Jenny's shoulder. "I guess we'll stay for a while, Duke Wolfrik. But only a short while. My daughter is too young to stay up until all hours."

"You can always stay over," Wolfrik said glibly. "And please, Madam Jeeter, how many times must I ask you to call me Otto?"

Fargo read volumes in the duke's hungry gaze. Wolfrik's eyes feasted on Mary's ripe contours like those of a half-starved man on a sumptuous banquet. He couldn't understand why Mary encouraged the man by agreeing to stay a while. Cradling the Henry, he crossed to a high-backed chair in a corner. From it he could watch the doorway, the windows, and the duke all at the same time.

Wolfrik selected a chair for himself and dragged it over close to Mary and Jenny. "Now then, suppose you tell me how it is you invited Mr. Fargo to your house for supper this evening?"

Fargo answered first. "It doesn't concern you."

"I must respectfully disagree," Wolfrik said civilly enough. "I have made no secret of my deep affection for Mary and her daughter. Their welfare is of paramount importance to me. So when William Travers showed up and informed me she had taken a troublemaker into her home, I was naturally disturbed."

"Billy was the one?" Mary said.

"A commendable young man," Duke Wolfrik stated. "If all the citizens of my town were as conscientious as he is there wouldn't be nearly as much griping."

"Conscientious, hell," Fargo said. "He did it because he wants Mary for himself, and he was jealous."

"Eh?" Wolfrik's sunny disposition disappeared. "What's that you say? Mr. Travers has designs on Mrs. Jeeter?" He swung toward her. "Is this true? Has Travers shown an interest in you?"

Mary shrugged. "He's made a few comments, but he's harmless enough."

For a fleeting instant Duke Otto Wolfrik's face mirrored raw, unbridled hatred. His features became contorted with rage so potent, he turned scarlet from his neck to the top of his bald pate. But it only lasted an instant. Then, exercising extraordinary self-control, he composed himself and commented, "I imagine I shouldn't blame the young man. You are, after all, a stunning beauty."

The compliment embarrassed Mary. "Please don't make an issue of it. Billy's never stepped out of line or been rude to me."

"What about that time Billy got hold of your arm and wouldn't let go?" Jenny innocently interjected.

"How's that, child?" Duke Wolfrik asked.

"It was that time a month or so ago when you took us on a picnic," Jenny related. "Billy was waiting for us when we got back and he was real mad at ma."

"You don't say."

Mary leaned over to rest a hand on the duke's gold-trimmed cuff. "Please. It's nothing. I don't want you to make a fuss on my account."

A flash of insight filled Fargo. She was speaking up for Travers because she was scared of what the duke might do to him.

"Perish the thought, my dear woman," Wolfrik said. He put his hand on hers, but she pulled away, eliciting a frown. "Is my touch so distasteful?"

"Not at all," Mary answered. "I just don't want to mislead you."

"I know, I know," Duke Wolfrik said irritably. "You keep telling me you are not ready to commit to another man. The memory of your husband's death is too fresh in your mind."

"And it is," Mary stressed.

Wolfrik rose and stepped to a window. "I wonder if you appreciate the irony. In my native Transia I could have my pick of any woman I wanted." He jabbed a thumb at the pane. "Only here, in this barbaric land of logic run amok, would my wealth, power and prestige count for naught."

"If you hate this country so much," Fargo said to change the subject and spare Mary further criticism, "why did you move here? Why did you build your own town?"

"Valid questions," Duke Wolfrik said. "I must have given you the wrong impression. Yes, your country is wretchedly savage. Yes, your government is woefully misguided. But for all that I love it here." Wolfrik turned, aglow with sincerity. "I love the thrill of creating order from this chaos. I love the excitement of carving an empire from virgin wilderness. The challenges, the hardships, they inspire me."

"Damned if you aren't serious," Fargo said.

"Why wouldn't I be?" Duke Wolfrik moved to the mantle. "America is like the serpents in these jars." He tapped one and the glass buzzed. "Primitive. Untamed. Dangerous. Everything Transia is not."

"But I thought you're an important man there," Mary mentioned.

"I am. Transia is the motherland, the fount from which the Wolfrik's have sprung for untold generations." The duke dropped back into his chair. "Our citizens are peaceful and happy. Our cities are clean and prosperous. People can walk the streets at any time of the day or night and feel perfectly safe." His voice dropped and he said sadly, "Transia is a model country, and the single most boring place on the planet."

Mary disagreed. "It sounds like paradise."

"A prison would be more apt," Wolfrik lamented. "Day after day I attended dull formal ceremonies. Night after night I went to balls or the theater. My life was wasting away while I gave speeches and listened to endless talk about the latest fashions and the most popular poets." Clenching his hands, he hissed like one of the rattlers. "The monotony was unbearable. It became more than I could tolerate. So when the king asked me to conduct a tour of America and seek business opportunities on your shores, as other countries are doing, I leaped at the chance."

Fargo was being shown a whole new aspect to the man. "Was the town his idea or yours?"

"The whole enterprise is my brainchild," Wolfrik declared. "I foresee a great demand for cattle in the not-too-distant future. By then I will have half a million head ready for market, and when I sell them I will quadruple my government's investment."

"But you're not doing it for the money?" Mary said.

"My dear woman, money is of no consequence. I'm doing this for the challenge, for the thrill."

Fargo was more interested in something else the duke had mentioned. "You expect to have half a million cattle?"

The butler chose that moment to arrive bearing a silver tray carrying their refreshments. Mary accepted a cup of steaming tea, balancing the saucer on her knee. Jenny tried to pretend she wasn't interested in the hot chocolate by turning away, and the butler deposited it on a mahogany end table beside the sofa. She resisted the tempting odor for all of fifteen seconds, then scooped up the cup and sipped loudly, smacking her lips when she was done.

Fargo's whiskey was the same brand Fetterman had brought to him at the hotel. He wet his throat, waiting for the duke to answer his question, which Wolfrik did once the butler

61

finished serving and moved over by the door to await further instructions.

"Yes, Mr. Fargo. You heard correctly. Half a million. I already have twenty thousand, and I've sent buyers to Texas and elsewhere to acquire the rest. They will be driven here in large herds over the next year and a half. When the boom market develops, as I predict it will, I will be in the unique position of being able to supply practically all the beef the market will bear." The duke smiled. "A monopoly, I believe you call it."

Fargo tried to envision how much acreage would be needed to feed and support half a million hungry cows. "You'd need to own most of the land from here to Denver," he said. Land claimed by the Flatheads, the Blackfeet, the Sioux and others.

"Ultimately I will."

"You can't be serious," Fargo said flatly.

"Why not?" Duke Wolfrik took a swallow of brandy from an ivory-inlaid stein the butler had handed him. "Savages occupy the land now. Once I've driven them off, I can lay claim to all the territory I require."

Fargo laughed. "You're going to drive off half a dozen tribes with forty Imperial Guardsmen?" The notion was ridiculous.

"I have forty at the moment," Duke Wolfrik said, "but in six months another hundred are due to arrive from Transia. They bring with them a dozen field pieces, the most modern artillery ever known, along with mortars and dozens of cases of grenades." He swallowed more brandy. "I think that will be sufficient to rout any who dare oppose my designs."

"Our government won't let you bring cannons and the like into our country," Mary said.

"How naive you are, my dear," the duke responded. "Your secretary of state has bent over backward to smooth things over for me. As an official representative of the Transian government I am entitled to special treatment."

Jenny stopped savoring her chocolate long enough to ask, "Where is Transia, anyway?"

"Transia is a small mountainous country bordering Germany. Although small, our army is second to none."

Fargo was thinking of the destruction a dozen field pieces would rain down on an unsuspecting Indian village, and the carnage a sizeable force equipped with mortars and grenades could wreak. The Indians wouldn't stand a chance unless they caught the duke's men in dense woodland where the artillery and mortars would be useless. He realized Wolfrik was staring at him, and looked up.

"I can tell the full implications have sunk in. My grand scheme doesn't sound so far-fetched now, does it?"

"You'll end up killing hundreds of Indians."

"Thousands, I should think. Perhaps tens of thousands. It depends on how stubborn they are."

Mary was appalled. "Yet you sat there and called *us* barbaric?"

"Oh, please. Let us be mature about this, shall we?" Her comment had struck a nerve. Wolfrik was angry. "We are talking about primitives who live like animals. I visited one of their villages. I saw with my own eyes how they live in crude tents made of buffalo hide, whole families crammed together like dogs in a kennel. I saw naked children rolling in dirt, women and men dressed in plain deerskin. I took part in a ritual where they passed a pipe and called on their pagan gods for guidance."

"Their beliefs are different than white beliefs," Fargo said. "So what?"

"So that makes them inferior. They are uncivilized and uncouth. They can never fit into our world. The humane thing to do is eliminate them from it."

Fargo almost threw the whiskey in Wolfrik's face. "That's your answer? Extermination?"

"Not just mine. Representatives of your own government have gone on record as saying the only way to deal with the Indian problem is to crush them." The duke drained his stein, then grinned good-naturedly. "It is the law of life. Study human history. From the dawn of time superior cultures have always subjugated inferior ones. The moment the first Pilgrim set foot on this continent the fate of the red man was sealed."

"I'm not an Indian-hater," Mary said. "I refuse to believe our two peoples can't live in peace."

"I admire your compassion, but it is grossly misplaced. Save it for your own kind. I daresay, were you to be taken captive by these savages you feel so sorry for, they would inflict a fate worse than death. Many Indians hate us as much as most whites hate them."

The duke had a point, but Fargo agreed with Mary. "Killing is never the answer. I don't care which side does it."

"Speaking of which," Duke Wolfrik said, "I take it you're aware the savages attacked Sergeant Dieter's detail? At this very moment two Guardsmen are in the infirmary being attended by my personal physician. One is in critical condition."

"I was there," Fargo said.

"Then you know the cowards shot my men from ambush. Tomorrow I intend to send out a detachment of Guardsmen to hunt the heathens down and repay them in kind. I would like for you to accompany my men."

"No."

Duke Wolfrik was displeased. "Why not? Your skills as a tracker would be invaluable. Help us squash the vermin before they spill more blood."

"These vermin, as you call them, are Flatheads, and until you came along they were peaceful. Why are they suddenly up in arms?

"How should I know? They have resented my presence since I first arrived. But they have bitten off more than they can chew, as your expression goes."

Disgusted, Fargo rose and set the glass of whiskey on the end table. "I won't be party to wiping out friendly Indians." Cradling the Henry, he motioned to Mary. "It's getting late. I'm ready to leave if you are."

"By all means." Mary stood, pulling Jenny up beside her. "Thank you for your gracious hospitality, Duke Wolfrik. We'll be seeing you."

"Count on it, madam." The duke stood. "I'll have a squad of Guardsmen escort you back to town."

"That's not necessary," Fargo told him.

"But I insist." Wolfrik said, adding suavely, "And I think you will find that I always have my way." He paused. "*Always.*"

6

Sergeant Dieter and a dozen Blues accompanied them. Dieter requested that Fargo and the Jeeters ride at the center of the column so the soldiers could better protect them if they were set upon, and Fargo didn't object. Not when the war party might still be in the area and out to avenge the warrior who had been shot.

The ride, though, was uneventful.

Most of the lights in Wolfrik were out, and the town lay quiet and dark. The two Blues left behind by Dieter were waiting in front of the hotel. They shot venomous glances at Fargo as the sergeant directed them to fall in on foot behind the column until it arrived at the Jeeter residence, at which time they reclaimed the mounts Mary and Jenny had used.

Fargo was hoping Mary would invite him in for a cup of coffee, but she bid him good night and hustled her daughter indoors.

"Now it is your turn," Sergeant Dieter said. "We will see you to your hotel room."

"Like hell you will," Fargo said. He suspected the sergeant was under orders from the duke. "I don't need a babysitter. I'm bedding down my horse and turning in on my own. If you try to follow me, the duke's physician will have a lot more patients on his hands."

Dieter glanced at the Jeeter house, at their closed front door. "Very well. Just be sure you go straight to the hotel." At a wave of his arm the Blues performed a column-right and trotted off the way they had come.

Fargo clucked to the stallion. He had to knock several times before the stableman, Timmons, shuffled from the back room in his long underwear and a woolen nightcap to slide the bar aside.

"I ought to charge you extra for getting me out of bed so late."

"The duke was in a gabby mood," Fargo said, leading the Ovaro to the stall. "About talked my ears off."

"You had a visit with Duke Wolfrik," Timmons blinked. "Tarnation. All the time I've been here, he never once invited me to his spread. Is his house everything folks say it is? Big and clean and all?"

"Big enough to get lost in." Fargo began stripping the saddle. "And you could eat off the floors if you wanted."

"Land sakes. What about his stable? How does it compare to mine?"

"I couldn't say. I didn't go in." Fargo hung the saddle over a rail and removed the saddle blanket.

"Wouldn't it be something to have as much money as he does?" Timmons asked. "To have all those Blues at your beck and call?" He scratched an armpit. "Some folks are born lucky, I reckon. Me, I've been shoveling horseshit since I was old enough to walk, and knowing my luck, when I get to heaven I'll be shoveling heaps more."

Fargo suppressed a laugh to avoid offending him. "Maybe not. From what I hear, angels don't need horses to get around."

"How do you mean?"

"I heard a parson say they have wings."

"That's right! I plumb forgot!" Timmons beamed. "They fly everywhere, huh? So I've got nothing to worry about unless they leave messes all over the place like birds do."

Fargo hung his bridle from a hook and gave the pinto a last pat. "I'll be back at sunup. I need to leave early."

"No problem. I'm always up before the cock crows anyhow."

Shouldering his saddlebags, his bedroll under his left arm, Fargo shucked the Henry and bid the man good night. The general store, the billiard hall, the shoemaker's, they were all closed. The lights in the Jeeter home were out and he assumed Mary and Jenny had turned in. But as he passed their picket fence a figure moved from among the rosebushes and whispered his name.

"Hold up a second. I've been waiting for you to go by." Mary Jeeter wore a white nightgown that accented her female contours and swished against her thighs as she walked. "I wanted to thank you for all the trouble you went to on our behalf."

"My offer still holds. If you want out, I'll help you."

"I'm tempted. So tempted. But I don't want you to suffer on our account." Mary glanced both ways. "I also was hoping"—she paused, hesitant, then blurted it out—"I was hoping you'd see fit to come in for some coffee. Or whatever you might prefer."

What Fargo preferred most was under her nightgown. "Give me five minutes. Leave the back door unlocked."

"I'll be waiting."

Inwardly smiling at the prospect, Fargo walked on. He scanned every window, every doorway, but saw no one spying on him. When he came to the hotel porch he deliberately dropped his bedroll as he went up the steps and pretended not to notice. At the top he made a show of realizing it was missing, and turned.

Fargo slowly descended, as if he were tired. From under his hat brim he surveyed the benighted valley, and halfway down he spotted a line of mounted men less than two hundred yards to the northwest, watching him.

The Blues. Fargo had thought it strange of Sergeant Dieter to give in so easily. He'd had a hunch the duke had instructed Dieter to be sure he went to the hotel, and as fanatically loyal as Dieter was, he had swung around to the south to await Fargo's arrival.

Stooping, Fargo reclaimed his bedroll and made another show of yawning and stretching as he climbed to the porch and went inside. A single lantern had been left burning low over the front desk. Otherwise the hotel was as dark as the homes and businesses. Milo Fetterman had apparently turned in.

Fargo walked down the hall but only went a few feet before he crouched, placed his saddlebags and the bedroll down, and scooted over to the west window for a look-see. Removing his hat, he raised his eyes to the sill.

The Guardsmen were riding off into the night.

Fargo gathered up his effects and strode to his room. The window was closed, proof Fetterman had been there since he left. Undoing the latch, he opened it, stuck a leg out and ducked through.

Rather than go around front, Fargo prowled past the rear of the intervening buildings until he came to the Jeeters'. He started to push on the gate, but the hinges squeaked so he hopped over the fence to avoid making more noise. As he reached for the back door it opened from within and pale light splashed over him.

"I thought maybe you might change your mind," Mary said. A red candle burned brightly in a bronze candle-holder she held overhead.

"Not likely," Fargo said. She closed the door behind him and he laid the rifle, saddlebags and bedroll on the kitchen table.

"What would you like? Coffee or something stronger? I have a flask secreted away in the living room."

Fargo took the candle-holder and placed it next to the Henry. She tensed when he wrapped an arm around her waist and pulled her close, molding her body to his.

"I wonder what's on your mind," Mary joked.

"You did say I could have whatever I preferred," Fargo reminded her, and kissed her full on the lips. Not long or hard, but sufficient to leave no doubt in her mind as to his true desire.

Mary arched an eyebrow. "I should tell you to leave. That's what a proper lady would do. What the duke would want."

"What do *you* want?"

For several seconds Mary was perfectly still. Then her arms drifted to his shoulders. "I've been alone so long. So very, god-awful long. I need to be held, Skye. I need to experience feelings I haven't felt since my husband died." Her breath was warm on his face as she brought her lips nearer to his. "I liked you the moment I set eyes on you. You stir me where no one has stirred me except my sweet Ed."

Fargo rubbed the small of her back, and lower. "That's nice to hear." His manhood twitched and a pleasant tingle shot up his spine.

"Hold me, Skye. Kiss me. Make me whole again."

No prompting was needed. Fargo fused his mouth to Mary's and her lips parted, her tongue meeting his in a silken dance. She tasted as sweet as honey. When he cupped her breasts and kneaded them, she uttered a tiny groan. Her carnal hunger was undeniable.

"What about Jenny?" Fargo asked when they broke apart. It wouldn't do to have the child walk in on them.

"She's sound asleep, but we can't make *too* much noise." Mary kissed his neck, his chin, his ear.

"Where's your bedroom?" Fargo asked.

"I have a better idea."

Mary took Fargo's hand and led him to a door on the left wall. It opened into a large pantry. Stored inside on shelves were canisters of herbs and spices, jars of preserved foods, and other items used in cooking and baking. She closed the door behind them, sheathing them in darkness.

"Here?" Fargo said skeptically. There was no place to sit, and the pantry wasn't quite spacious enough for them to lie down.

"Jenny is less apt to hear," Mary said, cuddling against him. "And I don't mind doing it standing up if you don't." Her soft lips found his throat and traveled to his ear.

Fargo wasn't about to quibble. He kissed her neck, her shoulder, while running his hands down her back to her firm buttocks. She wriggled as he moved her against a wall and sculpted his hard body to hers.

Mary gasped lightly when his fingers brushed between her legs. "Oh! It's been so long. You don't know what you're doing to me."

Fargo made no comment, but he knew exactly what he was doing. Her flesh yielded to his caresses, growing warmer to the touch as the minutes went by. He stroked her thighs, probed lightly between them, cupped a breast and squeezed.

"Ahhhh. Do it harder."

Fargo obliged, and Mary threw back her head and mewed. Her nails dug into his shoulders and her hips ground against him. Flowery perfume filled his nostrils as he licked her neck and sucked on an earlobe.

Suddenly Mary stiffened and pushed against his shoulders. "Did you just hear something?"

Lifting his head, Fargo listened but heard nothing. The house was quiet as could be. He commented to that effect, adding, "What is it you heard?"

"A faint sound," Mary said, and nervously laughed. "Maybe it was just my imagination. I'm worried sick my daughter will catch us."

Fargo didn't want her tensed up the whole time. She wouldn't enjoy herself nearly as much. "Want to go check on her?"

"No, there's really no need. She hasn't gotten up in the middle of the night since she was four or five. Not even for a drink of water." Mary traced a fingernail along his jaw. "Sorry to be so jumpy."

"It's all right," Fargo said, wanting to continue.

"This isn't easy for me," Mary said. "You're, the first man I've—" She caught herself. "Well, since my Ed went to his reward, you understand. I can't help feeling this is wrong, that I'm acting like a hussy."

"We all have needs," Fargo said.

"I know, I know." Mary's breath fluttered on his cheek as she loudly exhaled. "It's just that women are supposed to keep theirs pent-up inside and not throw themselves at every handsome son of a gun who strolls by."

"Which you don't." To keep her from prattling on, Fargo

71

covered her lips with his. She stiffened and put her palms on his shoulders as if to push him away, then slowly melted as his tongue entwined with hers and his hands kneaded her breasts like a sculptor kneading clay. Her breath grew hot with increasing need and she wound her fingers in his hair, bumping off his hat.

Fargo kissed her for the longest while, until she was squirming and panting in wanton hunger. Lowering a hand to her bosom, he pried at a row of small buttons, releasing them one by one to get at her hidden mounds. When the nightgown parted, he slipped a hand underneath. At the contact she cooed deep in her throat and delved her tongue deep into his mouth. Her breasts were twin peaks of perfection, full and round. They trembled slightly at his touch. He plied first one, then the other, massaging and tweaking and pulling on the nipples until they were as hard as nails.

Mary's slender fingers roamed up and down his back and on around his hips to his thighs. She stopped short of touching his manhood but rubbed his legs from hip to knee. When Fargo grasped her wrist and placed her palm on his rigid pole, she gasped.

"Ohhhhhhh!"

Mary froze. For several seconds Fargo thought he had gone too far too soon, and she would bolt out of there like a frightened fawn. But she soon relaxed and her fingertips slowly slid up and down his entire length.

"Goodness. You're so big," Mary breathed, a note of hunger in her voice. She folded her fingers around him lower down and her breathing became heavy with lust,

Bending at the knees, Fargo lowered his mouth to her right globe and inhaled the nipple. Rolling it on the tip of his tongue, he set her to quivering and her hand to gripping his member as if to pull it up into her. Taking her other nipple between his thumb and forefinger, he lightly pulled on it, then gave her breast a hard squeeze.

Mary's low moans filled the pantry. She was plainly trying not to make noise but couldn't help herself. Her legs parted when his left hand strayed to her knees and languidly started upward, hitching at her nightgown.

Sliding his forearm up and under, Fargo rubbed her inner thighs. His fingers caressed the smoothest of skin. The higher he went the hotter she was. He slid a finger close to her core but resisted the temptation to insert it. Not yet, he told himself, not until she was primed and ready to gush.

For long minutes Fargo lathered her heaving melons, rimming them repeatedly with his tongue and fingers. Mary pried at his gunbelt to loosen his buckskin shirt, then slid her own hands up and under, fondling his washboard abdomen and broad chest. Her lips switched from his right ear to his left and back again, her breath like molten steam.

"I want you so much," she said huskily.

Fargo shared her hankering, but he still held out. Anticipation always increased the pleasure of release, and when they exploded it was only fair she enjoyed it as much as he would. He wasn't one of those men who were only interested in satisfying their own urges. Which probably explained why women delighted in being intimate with him.

Mary raised her right leg, rubbing it against his, another indication of her intense craving. She hooked her ankle behind his calf and tugged his leg nearer.

Taking her by surprise, Fargo slid his forefinger along her moist slit, eliciting a sharp intake of breath. Her nails sank into his upper back and she locked her lips to his neck as he traced his finger back and forth, tantalizing her with the prospect of what was to come. With consummate slowness he inserted the tip of his finger into her womanhood and her wet walls enfolded it like a glove. He swirled his finger around and around and her walls rippled. Drawing it almost out, he lanced up inside, nearly burying his knuckle.

"Ohhhhh!" Mary arched up onto her toes, "Yes! Yes! Like that!"

Fargo pumped his finger up and down, the friction creating more heat. His thumb sought her tiny knob and at his touch she inadvertently cried out and spurted. In a frenzy she thrust against his hand, her womanhood contracting, her hips rocking rhythmically. His forearm was slick with her juices.

"More! Give me more!"

Sinking onto his knees, Fargo replaced his finger with his mouth. A musky scent wreathed him as he sucked and licked, his tongue gliding up into the wellspring of her being.

"Ah! Ah!" Mary exclaimed. "No one ever—!" Caught in the grip of a violent upheaval, she exploded a second time.

Fargo kept at it until his jaw was sore and the lower half of his face dripped with moisture. Rising, he unhitched his gun-belt, opened his pants, and exposed his organ. He could barely make Mary out in the dark, but he saw her eyes widen as he aligned his maleness with her nether opening.

"Lord, what you do to me."

Fargo rested his hands on her shoulders, braced his legs, and slowly fed himself up into her.

Mary threw back her head, her mouth parted wide, but she never uttered a peep. Her blond hair had spilled over her shoulders and her breasts gleamed palely, as inviting as ripe fruit.

Fargo kissed them while levering up and down on his toes. The combined effect drove Mary into throes of delirium. She tossed her head from side to side, her lush form quaking from orgasm after orgasm. At length her legs rose to wrap around his waist and her hands clung to his arms as if for dear life.

"I never—" Mary said.

Fargo took his sweet time. Again and again he drove up into her, pacing himself to last longer. Her mouth fused to his and the two of them climbed toward a mutual pinnacle. Her hands were everywhere, raking and scraping. He sucked on her sugary tongue and she returned the favor.

Abruptly, Mary leaned her forehead on his chin and whispered, "I'm close again, Skye. So very close to the biggest ever."

Fargo tried to delay the inevitable by thinking of something other than what they were doing but his body refused to be denied. A tight sensation built deep down. He was on the verge of erupting like a volcano.

Mary triggered their final onslaught of pure passion by attaining the brink ahead of him. "Now! Oh! Oh! I can't stand it!" She came and came, her body a piston, her legs like steel shackles.

Fargo burst at the seams. His vision spun as total ecstasy flowed through him. Immersed in sheer sweet bliss, he let himself go, ramming into her as if he were seeking to split her in half.

Together they swelled to the summit. Together they sailed over the brink. Time held no meaning, and the world around Fargo ceased to exist. He drifted in an inner ether, the pounding of his heart his only link to the land of the living. Gradually he drifted back to full awareness, to the pantry and the warm woman still wrapped around him and now softly sobbing.

"Are you all right?" Fargo asked.

"Never better," Mary whispered, and sobbed anew. "Thank you," she said, kissing him. "I'd almost forgotten what it was like." Her tears, then, were tears of gratitude, not regret at having made love.

No one could ever accuse Fargo of neglecting his sexual side. For him, coupling with a willing woman was one of life's supreme treats. It was as essential as breathing, and he would as soon die as go without.

Stepping aside to smooth her nightgown, Mary said to herself more than to him, "I can't believe I've gone so long without."

"Maybe it's time you gave some thought to finding a new husband," Fargo said, and was quick to mention, "My offer to help you get back to the States still holds. There are any number of men back there who would be proud to call your their wife."

"What about you? Can't I entice you to give up your wanderlust and settle down?"

Fargo had expected the question. "There's still a lot I

haven't seen, a lot I haven't done. Until I do, I reckon I'll always be on the go."

"Too bad," Mary said. "My intuition tells me you'd make a great husband and a fine father."

Busy adjusting his pants and his belt, Fargo opened the door enough to verify that the kitchen was empty. Opening it all the way, he let her walk out first, then retrieved his hat.

Mary stepped to the stove and inspected the contents of the coffeepot. "There's enough left for a couple of cups. Or do you have to leave right away?"

Fargo sensed she wanted to talk. Since he was in no particular hurry, he nodded and sank into a chair. Besides, he had a few questions he wanted to ask.

Mary commenced rekindling the fire by opening the stove and puffing on a handful of glowing embers. Once she had flames crackling, she added a few logs. Rising, she leaned against the counter and folded her arms. "I've been mulling over your gracious offer all evening."

"And?"

"I want nothing more than to leave Wolfrik. But I'm worried."

"About how safe it would be for Jenny and you?" Fargo surmised.

"No. About how safe it would be for you." Mary sighed. "The duke wouldn't take kindly to my leaving. If we're caught he'll assuredly punish you."

"Then we won't get caught." Fargo brimmed with confidence. The Blues didn't strike him as being especially adept at tracking and hunting and living off the land. He should be able to shake them with ease.

"I wish I shared your optimism. I could never forgive myself if anything happened to you. For that reason alone I'm extremely reluctant to agree."

"You have an even better reason to go," Fargo said.

"I do?"

"Your daughter."

Mary stepped to the stove to check on the fire, then gave a

start and glanced down the hall toward the front of the house. Fargo had heard it, too. The dull clomp of hooves in the street. A glance at the wall clock showed it was past ten.

"Who can that be?" Mary mused. "No one is supposed to be out after curfew."

Fargo was curious, too. They hurried into the millinery shop and over to the drapes covering a wide window. Mary carefully cracked them and they scanned the street from south to north. A group of Blues had reined up in front of a house farther down. Sergeant Dieter and a pair of brawny Guardsmen had dismounted and were marching up a walk to the front door.

Fargo realized that Dieter had never truly left. Apparently the squad had waited out in the high grass the whole while. "Who lives there?" he asked.

"The Keatings," Mary revealed. "They rent out the upper floor to several of the single men. Billy Travers and a couple of others."

Dieter pounded on the door. It was presently opened by a middle-aged man holding a lantern. Whatever the sergeant said caused him to scamper indoors and when he reappeared Billy Travers was at his side. Travers was half undressed but that didn't stop Dieter from having the two Guardsmen seize him by the arms and haul him toward the horses.

"Oh God," Mary said.

The young tough protested but he was roughly thrown onto a mount behind one of the Blues. Dieter climbed on his horse and the whole column swung around and headed north toward the duke's estate. As they filed by, the fear on Travers's swollen face was unmistakable.

"It's Otto's doing," Mary said. "He sent for Billy because of what you said out at the mansion about Billy being interested in me."

Fargo had guessed as much. "One less problem for you to fret about," he said, assuming she would be glad. But she wasn't.

"Billy can't help being young and headstrong. If he comes

to harm it'll be our fault." Mary gripped his arm. "You must do something."

"Like what?"

"Go after them. Don't let the duke hurt him. It's the only decent thing to do."

7

A lady friend of Skye Fargo's dragged him to church early one Sunday morning. For two hours he had sat through a sermon about forgiveness and turning the other cheek. At the conclusion everyone had pumped the preacher's arm and thanked him for a marvelous homily, but to Fargo's way of thinking they were woefully misguided.

Turning the other cheek was all well and good in cities back East, where no one went around armed, and violence was held in check by laws and lawmen. But on the frontier, where there were few laws and fewer tin stars, violence was a daily aspect of life. Outlaws, hostiles, and vicious beasts were constant threats. Turning the other cheek to any of them inevitably proved fatal.

Forgiveness was a luxury frontiersmen couldn't afford. Fargo had learned the lesson long ago and accepted it as part of wilderness life. When others tried to harm him he responded in kind and never lost sleep over it. The preacher would say it was wrong, but when forced to choose between killing or being killed, Fargo chose life every time.

Hardcases and toughs got what they deserved. In Fargo's opinion, fools like Billy Travers who caused trouble and took perverse delight in hurting others, deserved no forgiveness. When Mary Jeeter begged him to help the hothead, Fargo's initial inclination was to laugh in her pretty face. He had never been one to refuse a lady in distress, though. So it was that less than two minutes after the Blues rode out of Wolfrik that he found himself hurrying to the stable and muttering under his breath about how big an idiot he was for giving in.

The huge double doors were barred. Fargo knocked but there was no response so he pounded harder, setting some of the horses to nickering and stomping.

The interior glowed to lanternlight and crusty old Timmons hollered, "I'm coming! Hold your damn britches on!" The bar was removed and Timmons opened the lefthand door. "You again?"

"Me again," Fargo said, brushing by.

"Don't you ever sleep?" Timmons complained.

"I need to go out." Fargo dashed to the stallion's stall and put down his bedroll and saddlebags to saddle up.

Timmons was incredulous. "What the hell is the matter with you, mister? Are you plumb loco? Don't you know what time it is?"

"It can't be helped," Fargo said, throwing his saddle blanket over the Ovaro.

The stableman wasn't pacified. "Why can't you be like everyone else and do your ridin' during the day? Or are you one of those galoots who likes to stay up all night doing strange stuff like my cousin Harold? He's always gallivantin' off in the middle of the night. Lord knows where."

"If it were up to me I wouldn't be doing this," Fargo said.

"Who the hell else would it be up to?"

Fargo chose not to answer.

"I came here to get away from all the hustle and bustle of Kansas City," Timmons groused. "Folks there were forever wakin' me up at all times of the night and it got to be too much. I like a peaceable life. Try to keep that in mind the next time you get a hankerin' to exercise your animal." He impatiently tapped a foot until Fargo forked leather and reined toward the doors,

"I doubt I'll be back before daylight."

"Wouldn't do you any good if you were," Timmons replied, pushing on both doors. "Once I close these again they're stayin' closed for the rest of the night. You can bed down with the coyotes for all I care. Leastwise you won't keep spoilin' *their* sleep."

Fargo trotted northward, unsure what he would do when he overtook the Guardsmen. Dieter wouldn't stand for any meddling, and he didn't rate Billy Travers's life worth dying for.

A stiff breeze still blew, whipping Fargo's bandanna. The night was crystal clear, a myriad of stars sparkled like diamonds.

Fargo stifled a yawn as Wolfrik receded to his rear. The Blues were moving fast. He rode hard for minutes on end without catching sight of them. By his reckoning he had traveled over a mile when a scream shattered the tranquil countryside, a scream of terror and pain, the scream of a man in his death throes.

Spurring the pinto into a gallop, Fargo wedged his hat to his head, then dropped his hand to his Colt. Five hundred yards farther he came to a slight bend and swept around it only to haul on the reins when a prone figure appeared virtually under the stallion's flying hooves. Veering sharply, he narrowly avoided trampling it, and came to a stop.

No one else was around. The road ahead was clear. Springing from the saddle, Fargo rushed to the body and turned it over, guessing who it would be even as he did.

Sure enough, it was Billy Travers. He had been brutally slain and mutilated. A nasty gash rent his throat from ear to ear. His nose had been chopped off, his eyes gouged out. Copious amounts of thick dark blood poured from his gaping mouth, and leaning lower, Fargo ascertained his tongue had been removed.

Fargo was perplexed. The logical assumption was hostiles were to blame, that the Flatheads had struck again. But how had Travers fallen into their hands when minutes ago he was in Dieter's custody? And why, if the Flatheads had attacked the Blues, hadn't there been gunshots and the usual racket of a fight in progress?

Standing, Fargo twirled the Colt into its holster. The best he could do now was haul the corpse into the grass and let the townsfolk know where to claim Travers for proper burial. Sliding his hands under the dead man's shoulders, he dragged

81

the deceased a dozen feet. As he straightened the Ovaro whinnied in alarm.

Fargo whirled, but the three men the stallion had caught wind of were on him before he could blink. They were three Flatheads in buckskin, among them the tall warrior he had seen earlier. He stabbed for the Colt but a steely shoulder rammed into his gut, doubling him in half and thwarting his draw. He swung a punch that connected just as he was slammed onto his back, the warriors on top.

Fargo braced for the searing pain of knives being imbedded in his chest, but the Flatheads grabbed his wrists and legs, pinning him instead. In his mind's eye he saw ravaged features and imagined the warriors intended to do the same to him. Surging upward, he hurled one of them off, but the other two straddled his chest, their combined weight sufficient to drive him down again.

Grimly, silently, Fargo fought for his life. The tall warrior's face was inches away, the man's dark eyes slitted in steely determination. Fargo slammed a knee upward, but the tall Flathead never so much as flinched. Within moments the third one leaped back into the fray.

Fargo fought with a fury born of desperation. If he lost, he died. It was that simple. Wrenching his left wrist free, he landed a solid blow to the jaw of one of the other warriors. The man was rocked by the force but didn't go down.

Suddenly cold steel glinted dully. The tall Flathead pressed the razor tip of a bone-handled knife to Fargo's throat and snapped fiercely in English, "You not move!"

Fargo mimicked a log. The slightest pressure and he would be slit from ear to ear just as Travers had been. He didn't resist as the other two seized him by either arm and roughly jerked him upright.

The tall warrior held the knife rock-steady and studied Fargo closely, then moved the knife just enough to prick Fargo's skin. "Tell us where he be." His English was thickly accented but no more so than that spoken by some of the Blues.

"Where who is?" Fargo said as his arms were twisted behind his back.

"You know, white dog!" the tall Flathead growled. "Where they keep him?" He motioned as if to bury the blade in Fargo's chest. "Tell us or you hurt bad,"

"I don't have any damn idea what you're talking about," Fargo snapped, and for his honesty he was tripped and compelled to lie facedown in dirt while the warriors securely bound his wrists with strips of buckskin. His gunbelt was stripped off, his pockets were gone through, and he was yanked erect.

"We make you say before sun come," the tall warrior vowed, wagging the long blade. At a comment from him the other two shoved Fargo toward the road.

The Ovaro snorted but stood still as they threw Fargo across the saddle belly-down. A fourth Flathead appeared, leading four mounts, and the band soon headed west, the tall warrior bringing up the rear and leading the Ovaro by the reins.

Fargo twisted his head. None of the Flatheads were keeping an eye on him. They figured he was helpless but they could not have been more wrong. They had failed to frisk him for other weapons and their oversight would be his salvation. By bending his legs until the heels of his boots brushed his back, he brought the tops of his boots within reach of his hands. A few tugs of his pants leg was all it took to slide the cuff down far enough for him to slip his fingers up inside his right boot. The Arkansas toothpick was right where it should be, snug in its ankle sheath. He gingerly pried at the smooth hilt until it was loose and slowly drew it out.

Just then the Flatheads changed direction, bearing to the northwest. Fargo swayed, his legs swinging wide to one side, and he lost his hold on the knife. It started to slip and frantically he grabbed at the handle. He missed, but he was still able to trap it between his fingers and his leg and promptly covered it with his entire hand. Then he gripped the hilt firmly, holding the toothpick so the doubled-edged blade was pressed against the strips of buckskin binding his wrists.

The tall Flathead picked that moment to shift and glance back.

For a few nerve-racking seconds Fargo thought the man saw the toothpick, but the warrior merely frowned and faced front again. Fargo sawed at the buckskin, the toothpick shearing through the deerskin like a hot knife through wax. The loops parted and his arms were free. But that was only the first step. He had to wait for the right moment to make his move.

Sliding the toothpick between his wrists, Fargo pressed them tight to hide it and bided his time. It wouldn't be long, he hoped. The Flatheads were making for the foothills bordering the valley and would soon be amid dense forest.

Fargo intended to reclaim his guns. The second warrior in line had the Colt, the gunbelt looped over his shoulder. His Henry was in the hands of the third warrior. Retrieving them posed problems, but he wasn't about to light a shuck without them.

It wasn't all that long before murky woodland reared out of the gloom. The Flatheads wound in among the boles, the tall warrior moving a bit slower than the rest because he had to guide the pinto.

Fargo reversed his grip on the Arkansas toothpick and started to rise. Unexpectedly, a clearing broadened before them. Waiting in the center were four more Flatheads. He instantly slumped over the saddle, the toothpick clamped between his wrists. He couldn't try to escape with so many warriors so close, not when all he had was a knife. The newcomers crowded their mounts around the Ovaro, examining him. Thankfully, none noticed the buckskin strips were gone, and within a minute the warriors were underway again, continuing to the northwest as before.

Chafing with disappointment, Fargo was borne steadily deeper into the wilds. He thought they would end up at a Flathead village, but after an hour the warriors reined up on the grassy bank of a gurgling stream and climbed down. Two additional Flatheads were already there, younger men tending a small fire. A rabbit was roasting on a makeshift spit over the flames.

Fargo tensed his arms as two Flatheads came over and pulled him off the stallion. They propelled him toward the firelight and he stumbled and fell. In doing so he contrived to land on his side with his back to the woods so no one would notice the missing strips.

The tall warrior strode over and squatted. "We talk, white man. You tell us where find Gray Wolf, I maybe let you live."

"Never heard of the gent," Fargo said.

"You lie." The tall warrior frowned. Placing a finger to his beaded shirt, he said, "My name Iron Fist." He bunched his right hand. "I show you why," he said, and whipped his fist in a tight arc.

To call the pain excruciating didn't do it justice. Fargo ribs spiked with torment and he doubled over, breath whooshing from his lungs. He thought for a moment a few ribs had been fractured. Granite fingers closed on his windpipe and he was shaken as if he weighed no more than a feather.

"That just start, white man," Iron Fist said. "You tell where Gray Wolf be, yes? Or I hit many times."

"If I knew I'd say," Fargo said through gritted teeth.

Iron Fist sighed. "Whites all same. All lie. All steal. All kill." He made another fist and coiled his arm.

Fargo girded for the blow, but it did no good. Iron Fist's hand truly felt as if it were made of iron, attributable, he suspected, to the tall warrior's oversized knuckles. The knowledge didn't ease the pain or dampen his resentment. "Damn it!" he declared, unwilling to suffer more abuse. "I'm telling you the truth. I only arrived in town this afternoon. How would I know who Gray Wolf is?"

"You know. You helped bluecoats, I saw you."

"I was protecting the woman and her child," Fargo explained. "I didn't want them caught in a crossfire."

Iron Fist considered that a moment. "You not shoot Crooked Elk?" he said in disbelief.

"No, the soldiers did. All I did was knock him off his horse." Fargo's ribs protested as he slowly sat up. "I was following the bluecoats. They'd taken the woman and girl against their will at the orders of the man they work for."

"Wolfrik!" Iron Fist bitterly spat. "My people call him Hairless Snake."

Fargo had to admit the duke's features did have a serpentine cast. "You know of him, then?" he said.

Iron Fist's bronzed face clouded and he stared into the fire. "This Wolfrik, this Hairless Snake, he visit our village two moons ago. We fed him. We smoke pipe of peace." He said something to the rest of the Flatheads in their own tongue and all the warriors scowled and muttered.

"What did Wolfrik do?" Fargo goaded.

"He say all land his land. Say we must go. Say we not welcome." Iron Fist bared his teeth like a wolverine about to pounce. "*All land his land*! I tell him not so. I tell him my people hunt buffalo many winters. Always come Grass Moon and Flower Moon."

"I know," Fargo said. The Grass Moon and Flower Moon were the Indian equivalents of April and May, months when buffalo were most numerous in the region.

"But Wolfrik say we not come anymore," Iron Fist said. "He say we go or he make us go."

The duke's arrogance was beyond belief. Only Wolfrik, Fargo reflected, would be brash enough to take on an entire tribe with just forty soldiers as his disposal. Then again, more were on the way, along with the latest in European armaments.

"Our chief, Gray Wolf, tell him we stay," Iron Fist said. "Hairless Snake grow mad. He leave our village. Two sleeps later Gray Wolf vanish."

"Do you think Wolfrik had him killed?" Fargo wouldn't put it past the royal pain in the ass.

"No." Iron Fist's neck muscles twitched. "Wolfrik send bluecoat. Bluecoat tell us Wolfrik have Gray Wolf. Unless we go Wolfrik kill him."

"The duke took him hostage?" Fargo had heard of some

harebrained stunts in his time, but this one by Otto Wolfrik topped them all. Thanks to Wolfrik's stupidity open warfare loomed. If their leader came to harm, the Flatheads would swoop down out of the mountains and overrun every settlement and homestead for hundreds of miles.

"Bluecoat tell us Gray Wolf be sent back after my people go," Iron Fist disclosed. "So my people leave."

Fargo leaped to the only logical explanation for why the small band of warriors was still in the vicinity, and why they had been attacking whites over the past several months. "Wolfrik never released Gray Wolf?"

"Hairless Snake say he changed mind. Say he keep Gray Wolf so we no cause trouble." Iron Fist smacked his fists together, his huge knuckles cracking like twin hammers. "We not get chief soon, my people war on whites."

Hundreds would die, Fargo calculated. All to feed the duke's lust for excitement and power. "What makes you think Gray Wolf is still alive after all this time?"

"We go to Hairless Snake's lodge seven sleeps ago," Iron Fist said. "We tell him give us chief. He tell us come back later, Gray Wolf be there. But when we come back, Hairless Snake give us this." Iron Fist addressed a nearby warrior, who produced a parfleche. Reaching into the bag, Iron Fist removed something wrapped in elkhide. His mouth compressed to a thin slit as he unfolded the hide so Fargo could see what it contained.

A severed human finger lay in a ring of dried blood.

"This cut from Gray Wolf's hand," Iron Fist said. "Hairless Snake say next time it be Gray Wolf's head."

Fargo had suspected Duke Wolfrik possessed a cruel streak. Here was definite proof.

Iron Fist reached into the parfleche again and drew out a lock of long gray hair with a strip of skin attached. "This with finger."

Gray Wolf had been partially scalped! It was the worst thing Wolfrik could have done, an insult the tribe would never abide. "Yet you stuck around," Fargo remarked.

"If we go, Hairless Snake maybe kill Gray Wolf anyway," Iron Fist said. "So we stay. Maybe find chief on own."

"You're gambling with his life," Fargo noted. "The duke might murder him to spite you."

"I warn hairless one," Iron Fist said, reverently replacing the items in the parfleche. "I warn if Gray Wolf die, all Flatheads make war. Rub Bluecoats out."

"What did he say to that?" Fargo was curious to learn.

Iron Fist paused. "Him strange. He laugh at me. Say if we want war, he give us war. When he ready, he kill all Flatheads." A flinty gleam came into the tall warrior's eyes. "I like him try. There be many of my people. Only a few bluecoats."

For now, Fargo mused. But more were being sent, along with the artillery and arms Wolfrik had boasted of. By holding Gray Wolf captive, Wolfrik ensured that the Flatheads wouldn't rise up against him until it was too late, until the duke had enough men and armaments to slaughter them. "You have no idea where your chief is being held?"

"No. We watch great lodge. We watch soldiers. But we no see Gray Wolf." Iron Fist closed the parfleche. "So you tell us where he be."

"We're back to that again?" Fargo said. "How many times must I tell you I don't know?" To forestall a beating he went on. "Wolfrik is my enemy as much as yours. I might be inclined to help you, but not if you treat me like this. And not if you go around killing whites who have nothing to do with Wolfrik or your chief."

"We not kill other whites," Iron Fist said.

"What about the man I found in the road? And the prospector your people butchered a couple of moons ago?"

"Bluecoats kill man in road. We saw them. I not know man called pros-pec-tor."

Most whites would have accused Iron Fist of being a bald-faced liar, but Fargo believed him. Contrary to popular opinion, most Indians weren't natural-born liars and murderers. Most were as honest and decent as any white person. Iron Fist impressed him as being exceptionally so, and he responded, "Tell me what you saw."

"We follow bluecoats from Hairless Snake's lodge. They go white village, take white man from wooden lodge. They not go far and stop in road. Bluecoat who yell a lot climb down. Pull man off horse. They talk. Many loud words. Then bluecoat draw long knife, kill man. Cut nose off, cut out eyes, and leave. We wait. Want look at dead man. Then you come." Iron Fist shrugged. "Now we here."

Fargo bowed his head, deep in thought. From the description, Sergeant Dieter had done the honors, and to throw blame on the Flatheads he had mutilated the body. Undoubtedly all at Duke Wolfrik's orders. The duke saw Travers as a rival for Mary Jeeter's affection and had disposed of him. It all made sense. But what about the prospector? What had the gold-seeker done to deserve being turned into worm food?

"You say you want help us find Gray Wolf?" Iron Fist asked. "You help us get chief back?"

Fargo looked up. "Yes."

"Why?" Iron Fist was suspicious. "You not know us. You not owe us. Why you help us?"

"To prevent the blood of innocent people from being shed," Fargo answered honestly. "If war breaks out you'll be playing right into Wolfrik's hands. Your warriors will kill a lot of whites, but in the end they'll lose. More bluecoats are on the way, along with guns that shoot ten times as far as an arrow can be shot. With them, your tribe will be destroyed."

Iron Fist's brow furrowed. He imparted Fargo's words to the others and they talked excitedly among themselves until Iron Fist raised a hand for silence. "Wolfrik hates us so much?"

"He doesn't give a damn about your people one way or the other," Fargo said. "He's doing it for the land. He needs as much as he can get his hands on. If that means slaughtering hundreds of men, women and children, that's what he'll do."

Iron Fist slowly rose. "My people have word for man like him. It means his heart cold with evil."

Fargo nodded. "He has to be stopped. Together we can do it. So what do you say? Do you want my help or not?"

Instead of answering, Iron Fist drew his bone-handled knife. The blade gleamed in the firelight as he leaned down and looked deep into Fargo's eyes. "You speak with straight tongue?"

"I speak with a straight tongue."

Iron Fist gestured. "Turn. I cut you free."

"There's no need," Fargo said, and lowered his arms, the Arkansas toothpick in his right hand.

Some of the warriors reached for weapons, others lunged toward him, but Iron Fist stilled them with a wave. Gazing at the toothpick, he smiled and said, "You free whole time?"

"Most of it," Fargo admitted, standing.

Iron Fist chortled. "I like you, white man. You not like most your kind." He replaced his own knife. "I take your word. We let you go. You find where Hairless Snake have Gray Wolf for us."

"I'll do what I can," Fargo pledged. "But I'll need my Colt and my rifle." They were turned over to him without protest, although the warrior who had claimed the Henry was loathe to part with it. Fargo strapped the gunbelt around his waist, injected a round into the Henry's chamber, and walked to the Ovaro.

Iron Fist and most of the others followed. A few fingered bows and lances, making no attempt to conceal their distrust.

Fargo slid the rifle into its scabbard. Stepping into the stirrups, he raised the reins to depart, but the tall warrior placed a hand on his boot.

"Wait. What be your name? How whites call you?"

Fargo told him.

Iron Fist rolled it on his tongue, saying "Far-go" several times. Then he said, "Listen well, Far-go. You find Gray Wolf plenty fast. Our chief die, we fight all whites. We not care

90

guns shoot ten times as far as arrow fly. Many die both sides. Understand?"

Fargo understood, all right. If he failed, the northern Rockies and Plains would run red with blood.

8

Dawn broke chill and clear except for a fine mist that hung over the south end of the valley. At the north end, on a slope overlooking the mansion of Duke Otto Wolfrik, Skye Fargo bit into a piece of pemmican and watched smoke curl from the mansion's chimney. He had slept on the ground under a spruce, his saddle for a pillow. The Ovaro was in thick brush nearby where it couldn't be seen from below.

The way Fargo had it figured, Duke Wolfrik would want to keep Gray Wolf somewhere close, somewhere he could keep an eye on him. What better place than the estate, with the Imperial Guard always on hand?

But where, exactly? Fargo discounted the stable, outhouses, and small sheds as unlikely. Nor could he see Wolfrik imprisoning the chief in the barracks. So it was either the log building at the edge of the trees or the mansion itself, but on second thought he dismissed the mansion, as well. Wolfrik had a low opinion of Indians. The duke regarded them as simpleminded primitives, dirty and uncouth, and wouldn't keep one in his immaculate residence.

That left the log building.

Smoke was rising from the barracks chimney. A pair of Guardsmen emerged carrying buckets and walked around to the side where a pump was located, One worked the lever while the other held the buckets under the spout.

Fargo was more interested in a third Guardsman who came out and headed straight for the log structure. The man had a rifle slung over his shoulder and moved briskly. When he reached the door he glanced both ways, then inserted a key and went in.

Stuffing the last of the pemmican into a pocket, Fargo stood. Other than the sentries and the pair at the pump no one else was out and about yet. He couldn't ask for a better opportunity. Ducking low, he descended the slope, avoiding downed branches and twigs along the way, never once exposing himself to view.

Forty feet from the rear wall Fargo sank onto his stomach and crawled. Moving from trunk to trunk, he was close to the northwest corner when out of nowhere a sentry appeared, strolling toward him. His hand swooped to the Colt.

The Guardsman's rifle pointed idly at the ground. A flock of finches flitting about in the undergrowth seemed to amuse him, and he wasn't paying much attention to anything else.

Fargo didn't want to shoot if he could help it. He kept hoping the sentry would go around to the front of the building, but the man tramped toward the tree screening him. Silently pushing onto his knees, Fargo drew his revolver. The trunk wasn't all that wide, and the Blue was bound to spot him and shout an alarm. He slid to the right, keeping it between them, and steeled his legs to spring.

Chirping merrily, the finches winged away. The Blue smiled, then shouldered his rifle and gazed directly at the tree. A sudden widening of his eyes confirmed Fargo's prediction.

Uncoiling, Fargo leaped at the Guardsman as the man's mouth gaped to shout. Arcing the Colt's barrel up and around, he slammed it against the Blue's jaw. One blow buckled the soldier at the knees, a second sprawled him flat.

Quickly, Fargo ran to the corner and peered out to see if the commotion had been noticed. The pair of Guardsmen over by the pump were toting full buckets into the barracks. Of the sentries, only one was near the log building and he was fiddling with his uniform.

Fargo dashed to the opposite corner and worked toward the front, his back to the wall. There hadn't been any windows at the rear nor were there any on the side. Yet another indication it was ideal for housing a prisoner.

The door had been left slightly ajar. Fargo glanced at the mansion, at the barracks, at the stable, then hurtled toward the doorway as if fired from one of the duke's field pieces. Thankfully the hinges didn't creak as he slipped inside and side-stepped to the left so he wouldn't be silhouetted against the light for the brief second it took to swing the door near shut.

A narrow hall was flanked by four rooms, two on the right, two on the left. As Fargo moved toward them a vaguely familiar odor tingled his nose. An acrid scent, like that of coals in a fire. Black powder, he realized. Residue from a dozen casks of powder stacked in the first room he came to, along with crates of guns and ammunition.

The log buildings wasn't a prison. It was an armory.

From farther down came a cough. Fargo slipped into the room heartbeats before someone tromped toward the entrance. The Guardsman who had entered a while ago walked by, carrying an armful of cartridge belts. At the door he paused to grip the latch.

In long strides Fargo overtook him. Seizing the spike atop the man's metal helmet, he wrenched the helmet off and smashed the Colt over the Guardsman's head. So swiftly did he strike, the Blue sank unconscious on the floor without uttering a peep. Pivoting, Fargo inspected the rest of the rooms and discovered they were filled with arms and munitions. Duke Wolfrik already had enough to outfit a small army. When the rest arrived he'd need to build another building to hold it.

Keen disappointment pricked Fargo; Gray Wolf wasn't there. He moved toward the entrance, debating where to look next, then stopped, struck by an appealing notion. Going into the first room, he hefted one of the casks. It was sealed tight, but by stabbing the Arkansas toothpick into the plug and jerking hard, he soon had it open and upended it over the other casks and crates.

Duke Wolfrik's day was about to be ruined.

Fargo needed time to find the Flathead chief. Destroying

the duke's armory was bound to cause a hitch in Wolfrik's plans and possibly buy him all he needed.

When enough powder had been poured out, Fargo backed into the hall, leaving a black trail clear to the entrance. He cast the near-empty cask aside, gripped the Blue by the wrists, and used a foot to cautiously ease the door open. Confirming no one was anywhere near, he rolled the Guardsman outside.

Cocking the Colt, Fargo turned and held the muzzle next to the trail of powder. He'd have maybe twenty seconds before the casks ignited, if that. Undaunted, he squeezed the trigger.

The muzzle flash had the desired effect. Smoke and tiny flames crackled to life as Fargo rotated on a boot heel. Mentally counting the seconds, he grasped the Blue's arm and hauled him to the right, to the corner and past it.

Yells punctured the dawn, and sentries sprinted toward him. A shot cracked. Then another.

Fargo let go of the Guardsman and bounded toward the rear. In a few short moments the armory was going to go up like a fireworks display and he had to put as much distance as he could behind him. He flew around the next corner and sped toward the undergrowth.

The sentry he had knocked out was rising unsteadily, a hand pressed to a bloody jaw. The man saw him and staggered back against the building, out of fear for his life.

"Run like hell!" Fargo advised, and did just that, racing up the slope as if the hounds of the netherworld were nipping at his heels.

"Halt or I'll shoot!" The befuddled sentry fumbled at the flap covering his holster, drew his Beaumont-Adams .44, and tried to take aim. "Halt, I say!"

Fargo slanted to the right, putting a cluster of trees behind him to buffer the blast. He covered five more yards, his mental count at thirty, and he was beginning to think the black powder had sputtered out when a deafening explosion ripped the dawn.

The ground under Fargo shook as if to an earthquake and an invisible sledgehammer slammed into his back. The impact flung him a dozen yards into a thicket. He tumbled end over end, thin branches tearing at his face and neck, and came to rest on his back in a swirl of dust and brush. Blinking to clear his vision, he beheld the result of his handwork.

A spectacular fireball had boiled sixty or seventy feet into the sky and was billowing outward in vivid sheets of red and orange. Where the armory had stood roiled a cauldron of flame, scorching the earth for dozens of yards around. The logs had been blown to bits and were coalescing into a cloud of debris that would rain down as soon as the force of the blast expended itself.

Heaving to his feet, Fargo resumed his flight. The sentries were gawking in astonishment, while from the barracks rushed bewildered Guardsmen and from the mansion burst dumbfounded servants.

A rifle cracked as Fargo weaved among saplings. Next to him a bole thudded to the impact of a slug. One of the sentries had spotted him. The man hollered, and the next second three or four rifles opened up, the Blues peppering the vegetation as they sought to bring him down.

A bullet buzzed Fargo's right ear. Another nearly clipped his cheek.

Running flat-out, Fargo reached the Ovaro. He gripped the saddle horn and vaulted onto the horse, hugging it as he reined eastward. Guardsmen were speeding to head him off, but they the were all on foot. Fargo applied his spurs and the stallion burst into a headlong gallop as more slugs clipped leaves and gouged furrows in tree trunks on either side. He looked back and saw that Duke Otto Wolfrik had emerged from the mansion.

Attired in his pressed uniform with its glittering medals, his boots polished to a shine, his bald pate glistening in the morning sunlight, the duke stood with his hands on his hips, glaring right at him. Even at that distance there was no mistaking the bald rage twisting the duke's countenance.

Fargo had made a vicious enemy. The duke was bound to order the Blues to hunt him down and slay him. He had to stay one step ahead of them until he found Gray Wolf and averted open warfare with the Flatheads. But first a visit to town was called for. He had to fill Mary in on all that had happened since they parted company.

Holding to an easterly course until he was half a mile from the estate, Fargo reined to the south and climbed to the crest of the first hill he came to. None of the Blues had given chase, which puzzled him immensely. A thick column of black smoke still rose from the charred ruin of the armory, and many of the Guardsmen were running back and forth from the pump to the fire, toting buckets.

Fargo continued on toward town. The morning was clear and bright, the pristine wilderness alive with the musical warbling of birds, but he was too absorbed in the problems he faced to enjoy his surroundings. He pondered long and hard how best to go about thwarting the duke, and by the time Wolfrik rose up out of the waving grass like an island in the sea, he had come up with a plan.

The townspeople were going about their daily routines. Rather than go down the street and be seen by everyone, Fargo moved along the rear of the buildings to the Jeeter house and hitched the Ovaro to the white picket fence. He took the Henry with him. Mary had evidently been waiting for him to return because the instant he lightly knocked, she opened the door and pulled him indoors.

"I've heard the news." Mary had on a plain cotton dress with lace at the throat and sleeves. Over on the stove coffee percolated, the fragrance filling the kitchen.

"You did?" Fargo said, wondering which news she referred to. It couldn't be the destruction of the armory. No one could have beaten him to town.

"A couple of Blues showed up shortly after sunup. They posted a notice about Billy. It says he was butchered by Flatheads."

What with all that had transpired Fargo had almost forgotten about Travers. The duke hadn't wasted any time assigning blame, all part of the scheme to wipe out the Flatheads. "It wasn't Indians," Fargo said, selecting a chair. "How about a cup of coffee and I'll tell you all about it?" He paused. "Is Jenny up yet?"

"She's in the millinery. As part of her morning chores she has to sweep it out every morning before we open. We can talk freely."

Mary filled a cup and brought it over. She listened intently to all Fargo had to say and when he was done she sat back, appalled. "I never liked Otto much, but I had no idea he was such an inhuman monster. He doesn't care how many people die so long as he gets his way."

"Will you help me stop him?"

"How?" Mary responded. "I wouldn't be much use in a fight."

Fargo smiled. "I was thinking more along the lines of calling a town meeting so we can tell everyone what Wolfrik is up to. If we can get them to stand up to him—"

"You're asking a lot," Mary interrupted. "Half probably wouldn't come. Word has spread about you being a trouble-maker, remember?"

"We need to try." Fargo could think of several who would side with him, and he could use all their help convincing the others.

Mary rose, retrieved a shawl from a peg on the wall, and wrapped it around her slim shoulders. "Very well. I'll see what I can do. Mr. Fetterman over at the hotel is the one to talk to. He always calls meetings for the duke."

"He also has the key to the gun room, doesn't he?" Fargo recollected. They would need firearms if they were to have any hope of success.

"Yes. But he keeps it hidden so no one can get a gun without permission." Mary moved toward the hall but stopped when her pride and joy bounded into the room with a bouncing bundle of four-legged energy tagging along.

"Mr. Fargo! You're back!" Jenny squealed, and hopped up onto his lap as if it were the most natural thing in the world to do. "Samson and I were hoping we hadn't seen the last of you." She noticed her mother's shawl. "Where are you off to, Ma?"

"To see Mr. Fetterman. Fetch your wrap and we'll go together."

"Aw, I'd rather stay and jaw with Mr. Fargo."

Mary refused to take no for an answer. Mother and daughter left by the back door, and Samson plopped down with his nose to the jamb, whining in misery at being separated from Jenny.

No sooner did Fargo sit back down than someone pounded on the front door. Blues, he thought, and drawing his Colt, he went to investigate.

Luke Barstow, the burly blacksmith, was doing the pounding. Behind him were Frank Seaver, the storekeeper, and Seaver's son, Johnny. All three took a step back when Fargo yanked on the latch.

"You!" Barstow declared. "What the devil are you doing here? Haven't you caused the Jeeters enough trouble?"

Frank Seaver was more understanding. "We're sorry to bother Mary. We wanted to check on how she's doing. None of us liked it when the Blues dragged her off last night."

"The Blues also dragged Travers off and killed him," Fargo said.

The blacksmith's and storekeeper's were equally staggered. "We heard it was hostiles," the latter said.

"You've been lied to. The duke is trying to stir up a war." Fargo pointed at the hotel. "Mary went to ask Fetterman to call a town meeting. Once everyone learns the truth maybe we can put a stop to the bloodshed."

"Fetterman doesn't breathe unless the duke tells him to," Frank Seaver said. "You can't count on him. Luke and I will go from door to door and ask everyone to be here in half an hour. How would that be?"

Fargo told him it would be fine.

They turned to go, but Barstow hesitated. "About that fracas we had the other day. I was only thinking of the girl. The duke never liked her having a dog. We all knew the Blues stole it and left it in the woods to die."

"So you tried to stop me from bringing Samson back?"

"The Blues will only steal him again," Barstow said. "I didn't want Jenny to go through the same heartache twice. I figured I'd take the dog and hide it in my basement until we could work out how to smuggle it out of town without anyone the wiser."

Fargo looked at Seaver, who nodded. That explained why the storekeeper hadn't intervened. "Why didn't you just tell me?"

"We didn't know if we could trust you," Barstow said.

"For all we knew you worked for the duke," Seaver clarified. "He's had cattlemen and the like pay him visits."

"No hard feelings?" Luke Barstow asked, thrusting out his beefy hand.

"No hard feelings," Fargo confirmed, and shook. They hurried to round up Wolfrik's citizens and he returned to the kitchen to polish off the cup of coffee while it was still warm. The clock on the wall ticked loudly, the only sound in the entire house until a hubbub from the street again drew him to the front door.

Townsfolk were gathering. Men, women, and children lined the fence and half filled the street, with more coming from both directions. He counted nineteen, far short of the thirty-three total population. But ten minutes were left.

Mary and Jenny came up the boardwalk, Mary shaking her head to a barrage of questions hurled at her by the crowd. "What on earth is going on?" she inquired when Fargo opened the door. "Mr. Fetterman refused to call a town meeting without Duke Wolfrik's consent. And here I come home to find you've called one already?"

Fargo told her about the visit from Barstow and Seaver. Half an hour had elapsed by then, and he stepped outdoors. Twenty-eight people were present, among them Tom from the billiard hall, Old Ben, Travers's two friends, Mrs. McGillicutty, and a few other faces he recognized. They hushed when he appeared.

"I'll make this short," Fargo began. "Duke Otto Wolfrik is trying to stir up a war with the Flatheads. Unless you're willing to take a stand you'll be caught in the middle."

"Hold on there, mister," a man in a brown suit called out. "Who are you? And why should we take your word for anything?"

Fargo identified himself. Unfortunately, most of Wolfrik's inhabitants were from the East and hadn't heard of him. Out of common courtesy no one interrupted while he related his run-in with the Flatheads, but as soon as he wrapped it up a dozen people started talking at once. "One at a time," he directed.

The man in the brown suit hadn't been convinced. "You expect us to take your word on all this? Worse, you want us to take the word of *Indians*?"

A much older man agreed. "Redskins can't be trusted worth a lick. That Iron Fist fella was most likely lyin' to spare them from havin' their necks stretched when the army finally gets around to roundin' them up."

Mary spoke in Fargo's defense. "But what if he was telling the truth? If the duke doesn't hand their chief over the Flatheads will descend on us in force. We don't have enough men or guns to stand them off."

"Duke Wolfrik will protect us," a woman declared.

"With forty soldiers?" This from Frank Seaver. "I say we send a rider to the nearest army post, and until troops arrive we take up arms and defend ourselves."

"The duke wouldn't like that." Milo Fetterman had arrived and was pushing to the front. "We're not to avail ourselves of weapons without his express consent."

"Well, I for one don't intend to wait until I have a Flathead arrow stickin' from my chest to get his permission," Old Ben argued.

A debate ensued, and it was soon apparent to Fargo that only about half the town believed him. The rest had doubts.

About him, about the Flatheads, about the wisdom of taking up arms in general.

"If we don't lift a finger against the Indians they won't lift a finger against us," one man phrased it. "Even if Fargo here is right, and I'm not saying he is, their quarrel is with Duke Wolfrik, not with us."

"Precisely," a woman opined. "Our wisest course is to stay well out of it."

Disagreeing voices rose in anger and before long they were shouting at one another. Fargo waited for a lull and raised his arms to get their attention. "This is your town. Do as you want. But you're wrong if you think you can hide in your homes. The Flatheads won't stop with Wolfrik and his men. They'll sweep down out of the mountains by the hundreds, killing every white they get their hands on."

"You're only guessing," Tom from the billiard hall said. "There's no foretelling what heathens will do."

"Maybe we can arrange a truce," another man suggested. "Make it plain to them we're not involved and offer them trade goods to leave us be."

"A terrific notion, Paul," a woman agreed. "Give those savages a few blankets and trinkets and they'll be content."

Annoyance prickled Fargo like a rash. Unless they were mighty lucky, their ignorance would be the death of them. He couldn't help them unless they were willing to help themselves, but for the sake of the children he tried one more time. "The Flatheads want their chief back. Until the duke turns Gray Wolf over, they'll hold all whites to account."

"The duke knows what he's doing," a grizzled man remarked. "I trust him a hell of a lot more than I do you or some Injun. I'd bet a month's wages the Flatheads were the ones who rubbed Billy Travers out, not the Blues."

Frank Seaver was by the gate where everyone could see him. "You all know me," he said, raising a hand for attention. "You all know I'm a man of my word. I flatter myself you trust me so I pray you'll believe me when I say we can't afford to sit idly by and do nothing."

"Taking up arms isn't the answer," Fetterman said.

More heated exchanges resulted. Fargo had heard enough and went inside, his hopes dashed. They'd squabble and nit-pick for hours, and when all their spleens were vented they would be no closer to making a decision than they were right then. It was all on his shoulders now. He had to save the townspeople despite themselves.

Fargo poured himself another cup of coffee and leaned on the counter, contemplating his next move. It would take the better part of a week to reach a fort. By then the town and all its occupants might fall to Flathead lances and arrows. His only recourse was to find Gray Wolf before the Indians attacked.

Footsteps came down the hall. Not Mary's light tread, the heavier steps of a man. Fargo placed a hand on his Colt, but it was only Old Ben. "Were you able to convince them to come to their senses?"

Old Ben frowned. "We should thank the Good Lord for all the fools in the world. They make the rest of us appear down-right intelligent."

"Want a cup?" Fargo said, tapping the coffeepot.

"No thanks. I never drink anything stronger than liquor before noon." Cackling, Ben slapped a thigh. "I came in to thank you for trying to help us out of the pickle we're in. Most folks hereabouts are too pigheaded to appreciate what you're doing."

"I didn't tell them everything."

"Do I rate a listen? I promise not to blab to a soul." From a pocket Ben removed a block of wood partially whittled in the likeness of a horse. From another he took his folding knife and pried at the blade to open it.

"I blew up Duke Wolfrik's armory this morning," Fargo revealed.

Old Ben's jaw dropped. "You're joshin'? Without his guns and ammo, how's he to keep the Flatheads off our backs?"

"He still has plenty left," Fargo said. "The important thing is he'll think twice before he attacks the Flatheads until his reinforcements arrive from Europe."

"What reinforcements?" Ben asked. "Do you mean more Blues are comin' to our country? Hellfire, if any more show up, the duke can lay claim to half the land this side of the muddy Mississippi."

"That's the general idea." Fargo had more to divulge, but a shout from the street nipped their discussion in the bud. Mary was calling his name.

"I wouldn't get your hopes up, sonny," Old Ben joked as Fargo hurried by. "Too many of those blockheads worship the ground the duke walks on."

Mary yelled again as Fargo opened the door. "What is it?" he asked, venturing out. He wasn't expecting revolver muzzles to be pressed to either side of his head. Or to see Guardsmen arrayed the length of the street,

Sergeant Dieter stepped from the crowd, a pistol leveled at the Jeeters. "We meet again, American."

Fargo didn't dare go for his gun, not even when Duke Otto Wolfrik strolled up to him, smiled wickedly, and slugged him in the gut.

9

Rope bit into Skye Fargo's wrists, cutting off his circulation. Painful spasms lanced his abdomen, and his legs were scuffed and bruised from having been dragged into the middle of the street. Down on his knees under the blazing sun, he squinted at the townspeople lining the boardwalks and the twenty members of the Imperial Guard who had rifles trained on them. Another ten Guardsmen were still on horseback near the hotel, holding the rest of the mounts.

In front of him strode Duke Otto Wolfrik, the duke's burnished helmet ablaze with sunlight. "I can not begin to express how upset I am at the state of affairs," Wolfrik addressed the townsfolk.

Sergeant Dieter was a few yards away, his pistol pointed at Mary. A terror-stricken Jenny had both arms wrapped around her mother.

"You have betrayed me," Duke Wolfrik accused those assembled. "After all the money and time I invested to help each of you start a new life, you have turned against me."

Old Ben was the only one brave enough to respond. "Like hell. All we were doing was talkin' over what's best for everyone."

"Ah, but that's my point," Duke Wolfrik said sternly. "*I* decide what is best. All you need do is live as I say and your lives will be remarkably free from hardship and unpleasantness."

"Billy Travers might disagree," Ben said.

The duke's face acquired a scarlet tinge. "Mr. Travers was ambushed by Flatheads. I sent word to that effect at daybreak." He jabbed a thumb at Fargo. "What lies has this man been feeding you?"

Fetterman answered. "He claimed the hostiles had nothing to do with it, sir. He told everyone you had Travers murdered. He said you weren't to be trusted. And he wanted them to take up arms and oppose you."

"Did he indeed?" Duke Wolfrik said, his face growing redder. Lightning blazed in the gaze he bestowed on Fargo. "Have you no shame? I showed you the gracious hospitality of my home. I treated you as a friend. And how did you repay me? You blew up the building where I stored most of my powder and ammunition. Then you attempted to turn these good people against me. You're despicable."

Fargo saw a boot rising but couldn't avoid it. The toe caught him low in the sternum and he was slammed onto his back, the sky fragmenting in brilliant shards of blue and white as his chest pulsed with agony.

"Quit hurting him!" Mary cried and tried to take a step, but Sergeant Dieter grabbed her elbow.

Duke Wolfrik's eyebrows rose to meet the bottom edge of his helmet. "You too, Madam Jeeter? You would side with this man against me? Is there no end to the perfidy?" With an angry toss of his head, Wolfrik said loud enough for everyone to hear, "Effective immediately this town is under martial law. Guardsmen will patrol the street day and night. No one will be permitted outdoors without express permission."

"You can't do that," Frank Seaver said.

The duke snapped orders in Transian at a Guardsman a few feet from the storekeeper. Before Seaver could move, the Guardsman glided behind him and slammed the stock of a rifle into the small of his back. Seaver collapsed, writhing, and young Johnny tried to hit the Guardsman but was swatted aside like an annoying insect.

Duke Wolfrik showed no emotion whatsoever as he scanned the shocked onlookers. "Perhaps this demonstration will serve to remind you of your proper station in life. I am a noble of Transia, fourth in line to the crown. I can do whatever I please, whenever I please."

Seaver had his teeth clenched and was trying to stand but couldn't. Johnny was on his side, weeping.

"Imposing martial law is for your own benefit," Wolfrik stated. "The savages are stirred up and might attack at any time. We can better protect you if you aren't scattered all over the place."

"Why not give us our guns and let us protect ourselves?" Old Ben suggested.

"How many of you have ever fought Indians?" Wolfrik demanded, and when no one replied, he said, "I thought as much. Leave the fighting to the professionals. My men were selected from the ranks of the most experienced soldiers in my country. So I ask you, who better to safeguard you and your loved ones?"

Fetterman grinned and shouted, "Let's hear a rousing cheer of support for our friend and guardian, Duke Wolfrik!"

The suggestion was greeted by embarrassing silence. Stung, but striving to hide his feelings, Duke Wolfrik faced Fargo. "Let's turn to another matter. As a direct result of your treachery my entire enterprise is in jeopardy. So I think it only fair you redeem yourself by using your exceptional tracking skills to hunt down the band of Flatheads who have been plaguing me of late."

"Don't hold your breath."

Wolfrik motioned at a pair of Blues who none-too-gently pumped Fargo to his feet. "It wasn't a request. It was a command."

"You could break every bone in my body and I still wouldn't do it," Fargo said matter-of-factly.

"Undoubtedly so," Duke Wolfrik agreed. Lowering his voice so no one else could hear, he nodded at Mary and Jenny. "But what about them? Are you willing to stand by and watch that lovely woman and her precocious daughter be beaten until they grovel for mercy?"

Fargo's loathing of the man climbed to new heights. "I thought you liked Mary."

"She has a certain allure," Wolfrik said with lecherous zeal. "But don't think for a minute I wouldn't sacrifice her for the greater good." He smirked. "So what will it be? Either you cooperate or I hand them over to Dieter."

A good poker player always knew when to bluff and when to fold, and Fargo was a top hand at cards. "If I agree, you won't harm them?"

"You have my solemn promise," Duke Wolfrik said.

The duke's promise was as worthless to Fargo as teats on a bull, but he nodded anyway. "And you have mine," he said gravely. "When do you want me to start?"

"There is no time like the present. Isn't that the expression?" The duke snapped his fingers and one of the Blues flourished a saber and slashed the rope. The duke snapped his fingers a second time and Sergeant Dieter was there, standing at attention. "Sergeant, you will assign Corporal Treffen and five men to accompany Mr. Fargo in search of Iron Fist's bunch. They are not to let him out of their sight, and if he tries to slip away, they are to bring him back strapped over his saddle and gagged."

"Sir!" Dieter said. Pivoting on his boot heel, he jogged toward the soldiers on horseback.

Fargo rubbed his sore wrists, resisting an impulse to bend, whip out the toothpick, and plunge the knife into the duke's chest. The Blues would gun him down before the blade sank home.

Wolfrik motioned at the townspeople. "All of you will retire to your homes until this evening. By then a list of new rules will be posted at various points. Read them. Commit them to memory. Above all else, do not violate them or there will be severe repercussions."

"Just what we needed," Old Ben muttered. "More rules."

Like cowboys herding cattle toward a holding pen, the Blues herded everyone toward their homes. No one objected. No one resisted. Not when a dozen guns served the part of cattle prods. Not after the duke warned that anyone who balked would be shot where they stood.

In due course the street was deserted except for the Blues, their leader, and Fargo. Sergeant Dieter led six mounted Guardsmen over, one of whom, a stocky man with a neatly cropped beard, had hold of the Ovaro's reins.

"This is Corporal Treffen," Duke Wolfrik said. "You will answer to him until your return. He speaks adequate English so you will have no difficulty communicating."

"I'll need my pistol and rifle," Fargo said. They had been confiscated by Dieter when he stepped from the Jeeter house and he hadn't seen them since.

"What was it you said to me a couple of minutes ago?" Duke Wolfrik said. "Ah, yes. Don't hold your breath."

"Without weapons I can't defend myself," Fargo tried again.

"Without weapons you will have less incentive to try and escape," Wolfrik retorted. To Corporal Treffen he said in English, "If this man tries to get away you are to shoot him in a leg or an arm but not kill him. I reserve that honor for myself."

"Your wish is my command, sir," the corporal replied.

Resigned to going along, Fargo turned to the stallion.

"Not so fast," Duke Wolfrik said. "We have a few issues to discuss. First and foremost is why you blew up my armory. What purpose did it serve?"

Fargo didn't deem it wise to tell the truth. The duke was unaware of his talk with Iron Fist and he would like to keep it that way. If Wolfrik found out he had destroyed the munitions to hinder the duke's campaign against the Flatheads, Wolfrik would suspect where his true sympathies lay and might have second thoughts about sending him out with the corporal. And he really did want to go. The germ of a plan was taking shape, but to carry it out he needed to contact Iron Fist.

"I'm waiting," Wolfrik snapped.

"I wanted to keep you and your men occupied while I tried to convince the townspeople to take a stand against you," Fargo said.

"Why should you care what happens to these sheep?" Duke Wolfrik demanded.

"In our country we don't take our freedom lightly. What you've done is wrong. You've set yourself up as lord and master, and no one has that right."

"So you took it upon yourself to set things straight?" Wolfrik said in contempt. "You, a simple frontiersman, have seen fit to sit in judgment of me, a royal member of the exalted House of Wolfrik, the rulers of one of the oldest countries in all of Europe? In all the world? I would laugh were it not so pathetic."

Fargo gave it to him plain. "You must be stopped."

Duke Wolfrik studied him a moment. "Americans never cease to mystify and amuse me. You are all so naive, all so blind to the intricacies of the real world. Yet at the same time you are so nauseatingly self-righteous it churns my stomach."

Fargo was scanning the Blues for a sign of his rifle and revolver.

"If you insist on blaming someone, blame the people you are so concerned about. No one forced them to come here. They did it of their own free will and with full understanding of what would be required of them."

"They only thought they knew," Fargo said. "Now half of them want out, but you're keeping them here against their will."

"Half of them?" Duke Wolfrik repeated, surprised by the amount. "In any event, what they desire is irrelevant. They signed contracts."

Fargo looked at him. "You put a lot of stock in pieces of paper."

"It's all a matter of power," Wolfrik said. "Power wielded intelligently. Power honed over many centuries to a fine art. It is my natural right to rule others. My natural right to install myself as lord of the lower classes. To master them to my own ends."

"You honestly believe that, don't you?"

"Of course I do." Wolfrik pursed his lips. "And you honestly don't understand, do you? I was born to rule. My father was royalty. His father was royalty. His father before him, and on back for untold generations."

"So?" Fargo finally spotted his Colt and Henry. They were being held by a young Blue over near the Jeeter residence.

Duke Wolfrik snorted, "Typical of you lowly types. You dismiss hundreds of years of tradition as if they amounted to nothing."

"In America they do," Fargo said. "We don't like being treated like cattle."

"So you flatter yourselves," the duke debated him, "but the politicians in Washington have things well in hand. I saw with my own eyes how they manipulate your citizens. And I also saw that unlike the royal House of Wolfrik, they seldom have the best interests of the common man at heart."

"Justify it all you want," Fargo said. "You'll never change my mind."

Duke Wolfrik gestured. "What else should I expect from a man who runs around in deerhide clothes? Off with you! Track down the Flatheads as I have directed."

Three of the Blues behind Corporal Treffen drew their revolvers and pointed them at Fargo. Walking to the Ovaro, he raised a boot to a stirrup and swung up.

"Remember," Duke Wolfrik had to get in one last word, "if you give the corporal trouble, he is to bring you back so I can dispose of you at my leisure in the most painful manner possible." Wolfrik winked. "In the dungeon of the castle in which I was raised was a marvelous torture chamber. I became adept at applying the various devices, and I brought a few with me to your shores. If you misbehave I will gladly use them on you."

At a wave from the duke, Corporal Treffen reined the Guardsmen around and headed north. Fargo rode on the corporal's left. When they passed the last building he pointed at the emerald hills to the northwest. "That's where we'll find them."

"Lead on, American," the corporal said. "But remember. Try any tricks and we will not hesitate to shoot you."

"I want to find the Flatheads, as much as you do," Fargo responded. He was being truthful. The plan he had worked out called for their help, and Duke Wolfrik had unwittingly given him the means to convince them.

For the rest of the morning and early afternoon Fargo guided the Guardsmen toward the spot where he had last seen the Flatheads. When they reached the hills Corporal Treffen drew his own .44 and held it on Fargo as they filed through the trees. The clearing where the four Flatheads had been waiting for Iron Fist was empty, but the tracks the warhorses left convinced Treffen Fargo was indeed on their trail.

"You do well, American. These prints are not all that old."

Fargo pushed on. He hoped Iron Fist was still in the area. If not, there was no telling how long it would take to catch up to the war party. He kept looking for sign of them, but by midafternoon he arrived at the grassy bank beside the gurgling stream to find it deserted. Hoofprints and the charred remnants of the campfire were all that remained.

Corporal Treffen dismounted and signaled for the rest to do likewise. Hunkering, he poked at the embers with a finger. "This, too, is not all that old. By tomorrow the heathens will be in our gun sights."

Fargo stepped to the stream for a drink. As he sank onto a knee and dipped a hand into the cold, clear water, movement on the other side sent a ripple of anticipation up his spine. A painted face was peering at them from the depths of a thicket. It vanished the instant he saw it so he couldn't say whether it had been Iron Fist or one of the other Flatheads.

Cupping water, Fargo sipped a few times to moisten his dry throat. Then, speaking louder than he needed to, he said, "I'd feel a lot safer if I had a gun. The Flatheads don't know I'm being forced to do this."

Corporal Treffen had removed his helmet. He had dark, curly hair, clipped short as was Guardsman custom. "Under no circumstances will you be issued a sidearm. If we're attacked seek cover."

"How about a sword?" Fargo said. At close quarters it would serve in better stead than the toothpick.

"Not even a rock." From a jacket pocket Corporal Treffen took an embroidered handkerchief and mopped his brow. "I do not trust you, American. I do not *like* you. Were it up to me I would march you before a firing squad. But the duke seems to think you can be of some use to us yet so I must abide by his decision."

"Always the good soldier," Fargo commented.

"Always," Treffen said proudly. "I have spent most of my adult life in the glorious service of Duke Wolfrik and would gladly give my life for his if it were required of me."

Fargo perched on a log, his gaze roving over the woodland. If the Flatheads were there they were well concealed. "The duke isn't worth dying for."

"There you are wrong," Corporal Treffen said. "When a Guardsman dies in the line of duty he is honored above all others. His casket is borne along the streets of the capital, and he is buried with full military honors."

"That's in Transia," Fargo noted. "Here no one will give a damn, and maggots will eat your rotting flesh."

Treffen replaced his helmet. "Maybe so. But my wife will receive a pension for the rest of her life, and my son will be allowed to join the Imperial Guard when he comes of age."

Fargo was surprised but shouldn't have been. "You have a family?"

"Most Guardsmen do. My wife, Galiana, has borne us four children, my son and three daughters." The corporal smiled at the recollection. "We live in a hamlet called Ocksburg in the shadow of Mt. Kragen. Transia is a beautiful land, much like this only more picturesque."

Fargo thought of all the wives who would soon be widows, of all the children who would soon be fatherless, and he said, "Don't you want to see your country again? Don't you want to see your loved ones?"

Treffen was folding the handkerchief. "Why do you ask such ridiculous questions? When our replacements arrive we will be shipped home. Until then we make the best of this barbaric existence."

A twinge of regret pricked Fargo, but he dismissed it. The Imperial Guard had brought their fate upon themselves by their slavish devotion to the duke.

Corporal Treffen moved to his big bay. "Mount up, American. There is still a lot of daylight left and we must not waste it."

The Ovaro had its ears pricked toward a phalanx of fir trees ahead. Fargo looked but saw no one. Still, as he threaded through them he couldn't shake the feeling unseen eyes were watching. The forest was much too quiet, which he attributed to lurking Flatheads. Sunlight and shadow dappled the ground. Underfoot was a thick carpet of pine needles, on which the hoofs of their mounts thudded dully.

Corporal Treffen took his Beaumont-Adams out and rested it on his thigh, the hammer cocked. "This woodland reminds me of the Black Forest in Transia. The peasants believe it is the haunt of werewolves and vampires. At night they lock and bolt their doors and windows and won't let anyone in." He ducked under a low limb. "Do you Americans have similar superstitions?"

"We don't need make-believe creatures," Fargo said. "We have grizzlies."

"I have heard of them. Ferocious bears, are they not? With great humps on their shoulders and teeth as long as a man's hand." Treffen scanned the vegetation. "I would like to encounter one but have not had any luck."

"Trust me," Fargo said. "The last thing you want to tangle with is a griz."

And just like that, out of the brush on their left exploded a silver-tip, a young female with slavering jaws and raking claws. Growling hideously, she was in among the Guardsmen before they gathered their wits, raking a sorrel from neck to shoulder. The startled rider had his pistol out and snapped off a shot into the bear's face but the grizzly's thick skull deflected the slug and all it did was gouge a deep furrow. In another second the bear reared and swatted at the man, upending him from the saddle in a spray of scarlet.

Confusion reigned. Corporal Treffen and the others were shouting in panic and frantically seeking to take aim while their mounts plunged and reared under them.

The only horse not overcome by terror was the Ovaro. In the course of Fargo's travels he had frequent run-ins with bears, and the stallion had grown to rely on his control and judgement. A flick of the reins, and he sent it zigzagging off into the pines.

The Guardsmen were too preoccupied with saving their hides to try and stop him. Fargo saw the bear open another man from sternum to crotch, saw its steely jaws clamp onto a dun's neck as the horse squealed in abject fright. He congratulated himself on giving them the slip and grinned at the irony of it all. Then he rounded a wide trunk and in front of him was another bear, a cub born three or four months ago, and at sight of him it let out with a frightened bawl.

Fargo reined to the right to avoid a collision. As he swept past the cub a tremendous roar resounded, and he looked back to see the mother barreling after him, intent on ripping him to ribbons.

"Damn!" Fargo said, and lashed the stallion into a trot. The cub cowered in the grass, unharmed, but the mother bear didn't stop to check on it. She-bears were notoriously vicious when they thought their young ones were in peril, and this female was no exception. In a display of amazing speed that belied her enormous bulk, she rapidly gained on the fleeing stallion.

Fargo goaded the Ovaro to go faster. At a breakneck pace they flew through the forest, vaulting obstacles and avoiding deadfalls. The grizzly was twenty feet behind them then fifteen, then less than ten. A single misstep would prove costly.

The bear was beside itself. Her maw gaped wide, saliva caking her lower jaw. In a burst of speed she nearly overtook them and swiped at the stallion's rump but missed. The effort cost her a few yards, but she regained them rapidly.

Fargo kept thinking that at any moment she would give up and go back to her cub but that wasn't the case. Perhaps the head wound had incensed her beyond measure. Or maybe she was simply in a killing mood. Whatever the cause, she showed no inclination to stop and repeatedly nipped at the stallion's flying hooves, her huge teeth gnashing noisily.

The trees grew thicker, more tightly spaced. Fargo was hard-pressed to avoid them and the grizzly at the same time. Minutes later an open slope relieved one problem, but it also enabled the bear to go faster.

Fargo was a third of the way to the top when he realized talus littered the upper portion. Slippery, treacherous talus, a collection of loose rocks and earth that couldn't support a man's weight, let alone the weight of a horse. He would rather avoid it if he could, but with the bear so close he couldn't rein to either side.

Large boulders were just below the talus. Fargo spotted a gap between them and reined into the opening, his boots scraping as he shot through. Instead of an open stretch he found more boulders. To avoid them on the fly was next to impossible, but he did his best. He also tried to avoid the talus by angling wide to the right, but the grizzly suddenly appeared beside him, clawing at the Ovaro's side, compelling him to rein into the talus instead of away from it. Rocks and dirts cascaded out from under the pinto and it nearly lost its footing. It would have gone down had Fargo not hauled on the reins for all he was worth.

Only a few feet away the she-bear also slowed, her massive paws dislodging twice as much debris.

For long, anxious moments both animals flailed wildly. Then another jab of Fargo's spurs sent the Ovaro scrambling upward. He was ahead of the grizzly now, and the talus loosened by the stallion pelted the bear's head and shoulders.

The grizzly roared in frustration, floundering in her frenzied attempt to continue her pursuit. Not five seconds later her rear legs swept out from under her and she slid a dozen yards lower. Amid a cloud of dust and dirt she came to a lurching stop. When she rose her fury had abated and she stood and watched the pinto climb, then spun and headed down the mountain.

Fargo smiled. Drawing rein, he carefully dismounted and walked the rest of the way, leading the Ovaro. It was slower but safer. In a quarter of an hour he traversed the rest of the talus field. At the crest was a barren shelf, and there Fargo halted to let the stallion rest. He scoured the landscape below, but the Blues were nowhere to be seen. Inadvertently, the grizzly had done him a favor. He was safe now and could do as he pleased.

Fargo moved toward the opposite side of the shelf to scout a way down. A nicker from the stallion was his first inkling he wasn't out of danger. He looked in the same direction the pinto was gazing and saw the grizzly emerge from scrub growth bordering the east end of the shelf.

The she-bear hadn't given up. And in another few moments she would renew her attempt to tear him to pieces.

10

Grizzlies were famed for their formidable ferocity as well as their extraordinary tenacity. The mother bear was a living example. To her way of viewing things, Skye Fargo had tried to hurt her offspring. Now she was single-mindedly bent on sinking her fangs into him, and had cleverly taken another route to the top.

Fargo forked leather and went over the rim at a canter. More boulders were strewn about but nowhere near as many as before and there was no talus to contend with.

He was thirty yards below the shelf when the grizzly's massive form became silhouetted against the azure sky. A rumbling growl followed him into heavy timber where he paused to see whether she would keep coming.

The grizzly had started over the rim but halted. Indecisive, she swung her huge head back and forth. Maternal instinct at long last triumphed over bestial fury and with a parting snarl she was gone.

Fargo rode on, now and again checking behind him. He was still determined to contact the Flatheads, and to that end he looped wide around the ridge to avoid the she-bear and within an hour was back at the stream where he had glimpsed a painted face spying on the Blues. Venturing to the thicket, he detected smudge marks and a few partial prints. Only one warrior had been present, and had gone off on foot. But only to where a horse had been tethered well back from the stream. Once on it the warrior had galloped to the southwest. The Flathead had a substantial lead but Fargo was optimistic he could catch up by nightfall.

The afternoon waned, the hills reduced to flatland cut by numerous dry washes. The ground was hard and dry. Finding tracks was a challenge, but Fargo was one of the best there was at what he did.

The sun was balanced on the western horizon when Fargo spied a stick figure a mile ahead. Twilight descended, but still the lone warrior forged on. Fargo was counting on the man to lead him to Iron Fist so he was mildly confounded when he lost sight of him. Quickening his pace, he was a stone's throw from where he had seen the warrior last when a telltale glow drew him toward a steep-walled gully. Stopping forty feet out, he crept forward.

At the bottom, hunched over a small fire, was the Flathead, a middle-aged warrior with a bow and quiver slung across his back and a long knife in a beaded sheath on his left hip. The man had stopped for the night, Fargo realized. Now they wouldn't reach Iron Fist until the next day.

Fargo had two choices: make a cold camp and shadow the warrior in the morning or convince the Flathead to push on. He figured the man must be one of those who had been with Iron Fist the previous day and would know who he was. Taking a gamble, he held his arms out from his sides and stood. The Flathead wasn't particularly alert. A minute went by and the man didn't notice him, so Fargo coughed.

Whirling, the warrior whipped out his knife. He took several steps toward his horse but stopped when he saw Fargo wasn't threatening him.

"I don't suppose you speak the white man's tongue?"

The Flathead's blank expression was eloquent answer.

"How about sign language?" Fargo said, and resorted to it, his fingers flying fluently. Among the tribes who inhabited the northern and central Rockies and the ocean of prairie to the east, sign talk was nigh-universal. *Question: You called?* he asked.

Wary of a ruse, the warrior answered while still holding the knife. *Running Badger*, he signed.

Fargo's fingers flowed some more, saying, in effect, *I mean you no harm. Can you take me to Iron Fist? It is important I talk to him.*

I do not know where Iron Fist is, Running Badger responded. His eyes suddenly narrowed. *I saw you earlier in the mountains. You were with the bluecoats who seek to drive us from our land.*

Not by choice, Fargo signed. Full darkness was almost upon them, and he asked, *May I come down? I need your help if we are to stop the man your people call Hairless Snake.*

Come. Share my fire, Running Badger offered.

Half an hour of sign talk resulted in Fargo learning the warrior had not been among those with Iron Fist when he was captured. In fact, Running Badger had been at the nearest Flathead village, sent by Iron Fist to spread word that Duke Wolfrik wouldn't release their chief and to relay a request for all the warriors in the tribe to rendezvous with Iron Fist as soon as they could at a designated spot not far from Wolfrik's mansion.

Running Badger had returned to where Iron Fist was supposed to be waiting—by the stream—but Iron Fist was gone. When Running Badger heard the soldiers coming he hid in the thicket until they moved on. Now he was on his way to a secret place used by the Flatheads as a safe haven when they were in the region.

Fargo doubted Iron Fist would be there. In his opinion they were both wrong, and they should be looking for Iron Fist closer to the estate. *In the morning we should go to Hairless Snake's lodge*, he urged.

Running Badger agreed. He had urgent news to impart. Over eighty warriors from the first village were preparing for war and would meet Iron Fist at the agreed time. In addition, riders had been sent to other Flathead villages and hundreds more would soon be on the move. More than had ever gathered at any one time in more winters than the oldest Flathead could remember.

We will slay Hairless Snake and all who follow him, Running Badger signed.

And maybe a lot of innocents as well, Fargo mused, if the Flatheads caught up with the duke in town instead of at the mansion. The two of them stayed up until midnight discussing the crisis, then Fargo turned in. For a while he fitfully tossed and turned, too troubled to doze off. But he hadn't had a good night's sleep since he arrived in Wolfrik, and once he succumbed he slept undisturbed until a pink tinge suffused the east with the promise of a new day.

Running Badger was as eager as Fargo to get underway. The warrior's horse was a fine Appaloosa, well able to keep up with the Ovaro. He had obtained it in a trade from those master horsemen, the Nez Perce.

By noon they were close enough to the duke's estate to warrant caution. Fresh signs of Imperial Guard patrols were added incentive to hold to a walk and stop frequently to look and listen.

Fargo observed the estate from atop a hill west of the buildings. Only about two-thirds of the Guardsmen were there, including Corporal Treffen. The corporal and Sergeant Dieter were overseeing the construction of a new armory.

Duke Wolfrik himself put in an appearance shortly after the butler set silverware and plates on a hardwood table on the back patio. The duke strutted into the sunlight as if he owned the world, and the butler held a chair for him to sit in.

Fargo would have given anything to have the Henry. At that range a shot required supreme skill and more than a little luck, but he was game to try. Once Wolfrik was disposed of the Guardsmen would head East and that would be the end of the reign of terror.

Not long after, the rear door opened and out walked Mary and Jenny Jeeter. Wolfrik beckoned and they joined him at the table, but they were slow complying, and by Mary's posture she was none too happy about being there.

Fargo's irritation was boundless. He had assumed mother and daughter were safe in town. They were his friends, and he was obliged to sneak on down and be close at hand in case they needed him.

You should wait until night, Running Badger signed when Fargo let his intent be known.

No, Fargo couldn't. Every minute Mary was there, her life and the life of her child were in danger. The Flatheads weren't due to attack in force for several days yet but there was no telling if Iron Fist and those with him would wait that long. *Look after my horse for me,* he signed.

I will guard him as if he were my own.

Enough cover existed to screen Fargo until he was almost to the bottom of the slope, but reaching the mansion unseen was impossible. The pines that once grew close to the armory had been chopped down, and so had every tree within fifteen yards of the rest of the buildings. In addition, the number of sentries had been doubled.

The duke wasn't one to make the same mistake twice.

Snaking into high weeds, Fargo slowly parted the stems with his hands and inched along like a snail. Whenever the nearest guard glanced in his general direction he stopped. Soon he was as close to the rear patio as he could get.

A midday meal had been served. Duke Wolfrik was consuming his food with relish, smacking his lips and grunting like a hog at a trough, but Jenny merely picked at hers with a fork and Mary just stared into space. Glum and downcast, her hands remained meekly folded in her lap.

"Come now, madam," Wolfrik declared in his booming bass voice, "you need to eat. Or do you plan on starving to death to spite me?" He laughed uproariously, then stuffed a piece of veal into his mouth.

Mary's response wasn't loud enough for Fargo to hear.

"How many times must I repeat myself?" Wolfrik said irritably. "I brought the two of you here for your own safety. The Flatheads have been quite active of late. I expect that within the next month or so they will launch a full-scale offensive."

It would be a lot sooner than that, Fargo reflected. The reinforcements and armaments the duke was relying on would arrive much too late.

Again Mary spoke. Again, it was too softly for Fargo to tell what she said.

"Believe me, you're much safer here than in town. Thanks to your friend, Mr. Fargo, most of my ammunition and powder was destroyed, but not all of it. A supply is always kept in the barracks for ready use. More than enough to deal with the savages when they finally quit skulking about like the cowards they are and oppose me in the open." The duke lifted a crystal goblet and gulped what appeared to be either ale or beer. "I have a few surprises up my sleeve that will decisively turn the tide of battle in my favor."

Fargo glanced toward the barracks, wondering what the duke had that made him so sure he could defeat the Flatheads.

Mary raised her voice in anger. "But I don't want to be here! I'd rather be in town with my friends."

"Nonsense." Duke Wolfrik sliced into a baked potato.

"I resent being treated like one of your servants!" Mary declared, louder yet. "You can't boss me around like you do them! You have no right to treat me this way!"

Wolfrik didn't respond until he was done chewing and had swallowed. "My dear, sweet woman. How childish you can be. In time you will learn to accept the situation."

Mary half rose out of her chair. Madder than Fargo had ever seen her, she clawed her fingers and shook them at the duke. "Never! Not in a million years!"

Her spite startled Wolfrik, who lowered his fork and thoughtfully stared at her as she sank back down in despair, her chin drooping. "I had no idea you felt so strongly about it," he commented.

"That's because you never listen to me."

"Untrue, madam. I hang on your every word, your every gesture. Surely you realize I am smitten, as you Americans would say?" Wolfrik sat straighter. "Dare I say it aloud? Dare I voice the word no woman has ever heard from my lips?" He paused. "Mary, I am in love with you. Hopelessly, endlessly in love. And I will not let my love be denied."

Mary's temper flared anew. "But I don't love *you*."

Fargo feared the duke would be insulted and fly into a rage, but the man was as unpredictable as he was vicious.

"That, too, will change with time. Once this Indian matter is settled I promise to devote every waking moment to winning your heart and your hand."

Mary placed a palm on her forehead, the portrait of misery.

"This is a momentous occasion," Duke Wolfrik stated. "Never before have I professed my adoration of a female. A celebration is called for." Picking up a small golden bell, he rang it vigorously, and out of the mansion hustled the butler. "Velga, please bring a bottle of my favorite wine and two glasses. The lady and I have cause to celebrate."

"I don't want any," Mary said as the butler departed.

"You only think you don't, my dear," Duke Wolfrik said.

What happened next caught even Fargo by surprise. Mary rose up out of her chair, a steak knife in her hand, and flung herself at the duke. Her lovely face twitching in blind rage, she drove the knife toward his neck.

Transfixed with shock, Wolfrik didn't react until the blade was midway to his throat. Then he jerked aside, but not swiftly enough. The sharp edge nicked him, drawing blood. Lunging erect, he seized Mary's wrist, bent her arm backward so violently she cried out, and balled his other hand to strike her.

Fargo's own hand automatically dropped to his holster. His empty holster. He started to rise to run to her aid even though the sentries were bound to spot him, but the duke had paused.

Wolfrik glanced at his fist, then at Mary. His arm slowly sank. Casually, effortlessly, he wrested the steak knife from her grasp and stepped back. "My apologies, madam. Ordinarily I would never lift a finger against a member of the fairer gender. Please forgive my deplorable conduct."

"Forgive you?" Mary shook from the intensity of her emotion. "I *hate* you! Can't you get that through your thick head? I find you loathsome and hideous! You're a human slug, and I wish to God I'd never set eyes on you!"

Her outburst had a profound effect on Wolfrik. He looked her up and down as if seeing her for the first time, and said,

"You hate me? When all I have ever done is my utmost to treat you with special regard?"

"I don't want anything to do with you, Otto," Mary said bleakly. "In this country a woman has the right to choose whom she will be with."

"You Americans and your incessant talk about 'rights'!" Wolfrik hissed. "Very well. Never let it be said I can't admit when I am wrong. I thought I could win your heart, but I see now I was deluding myself."

Mary's lips moved but Fargo couldn't hear what she said.

"No need to rub it in," Wolfrik said, nodding at the back door. "If neither of you are hungry, feel free to go to your room. I'll have my men take you back to town tomorrow morning."

"Why not today?" Mary asked.

"Why not, indeed." The duke smacked the table. "Very well. Pack your bag and be ready to go within the hour." He turned his back to them and closed his eyes. "Now if you would be so kind, I very much would like to be alone."

Mary gathered up Jenny and went in, bestowing a last look of compassion on her misguided suitor. They passed the butler, who bore a silver tray supporting a wine bottle and long-stemmed glasses.

"Sir?"

"Forget the celebration, Velga," Duke Wolfrik said. "Send for Sergeant Dieter. I need to see him right away."

"Certainly, Your Grace."

Fargo was relieved Mary would finally be shed of the duke. Maybe Wolfrik would even permit her to return to the States now that any chance of a romance between them had been dashed. He began to back toward the trees, ever watchful of the sentries, then decided to wait and see what the duke had to say to Dieter.

The sergeant arrived promptly and snapped to attention. In keeping with the duke's edict to always use English, he said, "You sent for me, sir?"

Wolfrik was gazing eastward, absorbed in deep reflection. "Have you ever been insulted, Sergeant?"

"Sir?"

"Have you ever had someone insult all that you are, all that you stand for? Have you ever had someone treat you as if you were cattle dung?"

"No one would dare, sir," Sergeant Dieter said. "I would crush them where they stood. A man of honor can never let his honor be besmirched."

"We think alike, you and I," Duke Wolfrik said, facing his subordinate and grimly smiling. "Not two minutes ago Madam Jeeter saw fit to spurn me."

"No!"

"She truly has no inkling of the tremendous honor I was willing to bestow on her." Wolfrik's features hardened. "She not only spurned me, she told me that she hates me, Sergeant. She thinks I am despicable. I could see it in her eyes. I could feel it when she shrank from my touch."

"The woman is insane, sir."

"No, she's American. And I see now that Americans are inherently different from us. They lack our values, our wisdom. They lack Transian respect for the proper order of things." Duke Wolfrik scanned the windows overlooking the patio as if to assure himself no one was watching. "No man can endure an insult of the magnitude inflicted by Madam Jeeter."

"Do you want her disposed of, sir?" Sergeant Dieter asked.

The casual air with which the suggestion was made froze Fargo's blood in his veins. The sergeant wasn't a true soldier; he was a killer in a fancy uniform.

"Discreetly, yes," Duke Wolfrik said. "She and her child, both. I told them to be ready to leave within the hour. Take six of our most dependable Guardsmen along."

"Do you want me to mutilate her so the savages will take the blame as we did with Travers and the prospector?"

"Why not?" Duke Wolfrik smiled, and Sergeant Dieter saluted and pivoted to leave. "No, wait," the duke suddenly said. "I have a better idea." His smile broadened. "A stroke of genius, if I say so myself."

"Your brilliance is undeniable, sir."

"Instead of blaming it on the Flatheads, we'll blame it on the frontiersman. On Skye Fargo." Wolfrik chortled. "He's still out there. Still a thorn in my side. And you know what I do with thorns."

Sergeant Dieter nodded. "How do you want me to handle it, sir?"

"Fargo's weapons are in my study, take them with you. Halfway down the trail to town, shoot the bitch and her brat with his rifle and leave it at the scene to give the impression he dropped it when he rode off. No one in town owns a Henry and they all saw him carrying his around."

"Then you don't want the Jeeters mutilated?" Sergeant Dieter sounded disappointed.

"No, Sergeant. The townspeople are idiots, but even they would not believe Fargo capable of so heinous an act." Duke Wolfrik stroked his chin. "We will need to start a rumor. Something to explain why Fargo murdered them."

"Why not say she jilted him?" Sergeant Dieter suggested.

"As she jilted me? Yes, I like the irony." The duke clapped Dieter on the arm. "I can always count on you, can't I, Heinrich?"

"Always, sir," Dieter declared. "Your enemies are my enemies. Your will is my will. I live only to serve."

"Go select the men you will need and have mounts saddled," Duke Wolfrik directed. Again Dieter went to leave and again the duke stopped him, this time by saying, "Oh. One last thing. Shoot them in the back of the head. Make the deed that much more despicable so the cretins in town will want to hang Fargo when we catch him."

"Hang him, sir?"

"It's the custom in these parts, I'm told."

"And they call themselves civilized?" Sergeant Dieter joked.

Both men laughed and headed indoors.

Fargo didn't linger. Sliding backward until he reached the pines, he rose and swiftly climbed toward the crest. He intended to stop Dieter or die trying. Without guns his best bet was to lie in ambush and jump him. With Running Badger's help he should be able to get his hands on a pistol, and between the two of them dispose of the Blues.

Fargo had seldom met anyone as coldly calculating as Duke Otto Wolfrik. The man was worse than any hostile who ever lived. To Wolfrik human life was of no consequence. People were a means to an end, and when they no longer served a purpose they were disposed of as casually as if Wolfrik were crushing bugs.

Mary wasn't going to be one of them.

A shout from below brought Fargo to a halt. Thinking a sentry had spotted him, he ducked behind a spruce. But the Blue who yelled was in the corral attempting to saddle a horse that didn't want to be saddled. Another Guardsmen ran to help and between them they managed to throw a rope over its neck.

Fargo climbed higher, glancing over his shoulder every few yards. To the south the ribbon of road that linked the estate to town was empty. Cattle sprinkled the grassland bordering it. When he was near the top, he caught sight of the town, the buildings no bigger than the warts on a toad's back.

Only a few feet remained. Fargo figured Running Badger would be waiting for him, but he didn't see the warrior anywhere. As he cleared the top, his stomach bunched into a knot and an oath escaped him. The horses were gone! Running Badger had left him there and taken the Ovaro.

Tracks guided Fargo to the north side of the hill where the woods were heaviest. He looked and looked, but the Flathead and the horses were lost amid an endless green canopy. Foiled, he sat on a boulder and tried to make sense of the Flathead's betrayal. They had gotten along nicely, and Running Badger had impressed him as being sincere when they talked about working together to stop Wolfrik. Why, then, had the warrior stolen the Ovaro, stranding him?

The only conclusion Fargo could come to was that Running

Badger never entirely trusted him. Maybe Running Badger didn't believe he had met Iron Fist. Or that the Blues were as much his enemies as they were the tribe's. Now he was afoot, the toothpick his only weapon. Yet somehow he must stop Dieter from murdering Mary and Jenny.

Rising, Fargo ran to where he could see the corral. More horses were being saddled and Guardsmen were gathering at the rails. Soon they would be on their way to town.

Fargo headed down the hill, bearing to the southwest, his plan to reach the tall grass and swing toward the road. If he could get there ahead of the Blues, he would spring a little surprise. Increasing his speed, he bounded through the brush like a buck with a pack of wolves in pursuit. A log blocked his path and he vaulted it without breaking stride.

Fargo was halfway to the bottom when his left boot snagged on an exposed root. He tried to regain his balance but gravity wouldn't be denied. Momentum pitched him onto his face and swept him another ten feet to crash against a fir tree. His hat went flying, and for long seconds the world spun madly, the sky and the earth trading places. Nausea afflicted him, and it was all he could do to keep his eyes open.

For an anxious couple of minutes Fargo lay still, too disoriented to stand. When the queasiness faded, he jammed his hat back on and hastened on down the hill again, at a lurching jog. A large bump testified to how hard he had hit. He kept telling himself he couldn't quit, no matter what. The lives of two sweet people were at stake.

The trees thinned. Yonder Fargo beheld the tall, rippling grass. He had done it! All that was left was to get into position before the Blues reached him.

Then a horse whinnied, and a growl of bafflement rose from Fargo's throat. Sergeant Dieter and the escort were approaching much sooner than he had reckoned. Mary was next to Dieter, Jenny riding beside a private.

Fargo drew the toothpick. He had to try anyway. If he didn't, the Jeeters were done for.

11

Tucked at the knees, Skye Fargo sped into the tall grass. The Blues were sixty yards away and approaching at a brisk walk. Staying low, he angled toward the road. When he was near it he dropped onto his belly and snaked the final few yards. He held the Arkansas toothpick close to the ground so the sun wouldn't glint off the blade and give him away. Parting the stems, he peeked out.

Mary Jeeter was surveying majestic mountains to the west, blissfully ignorant of the dastardly fate Duke Wolfrik had in store for her and her child.

Soon Sergeant Dieter would bring the detail to a trot for the long ride to town. Fargo had to either stop them or slow them down enough for him to spring his surprise. To that end, he removed his hat and quickly tossed it into the middle of the road where Dieter couldn't fail to spot it.

Turning, Fargo crawled northward, paralleling the road for some fifteen yards. The ground under him drummed to the pounding of oncoming hooves. He flattened seconds before Sergeant Dieter and the Jeeters went by. For a moment he thought his ruse had failed and Dieter wouldn't spot his hat. Then a commanding shout rang out, and the sergeant flung up an arm and brought the troopers to a halt.

"What in the world is that doing there?" Sergeant Dieter said in surprise.

Mary leaned over her saddle horn for a better view. "Why, that's Mr. Fargo's hat, if I'm not mistaken. I ought to know. Hats are my business. No one else in town owns one quite like it."

"Most peculiar," Dieter said, and rose in his stirrups to survey the surrounding grassland.

The six Blues assigned to the escort detail weren't expecting trouble. They were only a couple of hundred yards from the mansion and they were complacent and careless. Not one detected Fargo as he rose into a crouch and glided around to the rear of the column. Not one saw him cat-foot up behind the last Guardsman on the right. Taking a long stride, he sprang onto the back of the man's horse, and as he alighted, he drove the toothpick's doubled-edged triangular tip into the base of the Blue's skull, just below the helmet, shearing through flesh, nerve endings, even bone. The soldier died without uttering an outcry.

The Guardsman on the left had seen. He was riveted in horror but only for a moment. Snatching at his holster flap, he bawled in Transian.

Fargo was already prying at the dead man's holster. He cleared leather first. Cocking the Beaumont-Adams, he extended his arm. Simultaneously, he shoved the dead trooper off.

Other Blues were shifting in their saddles.

Lead and smoke spewed from the muzzle of Fargo's revolver and the face of the man on his left spewed a shower of crimson gore. As the man toppled, Fargo clamped the hilt of the toothpick between his teeth and spurred his mount forward, between the next pair. He shot the Blue on the right between the eyes, swivelled and shot the Blue on the left in the chest. As the man fell Fargo grabbed his .44.

Now, a pistol in each hand, Fargo charged forward again. Surprise had given him the edge so far. But the next two had their revolvers out and were wheeling their animals to confront him. One snapped off a shot that missed. Fargo's answering round didn't. That left one last Guardsman, and Sergeant Dieter.

The sergeant jammed the Henry to his shoulder to fire. He had Fargo dead to rights but Mary abruptly lunged and gripped the barrel, deflecting it just as the Henry went off. The heavy slug meant for Fargo ripped into the last Guardsman instead, leaving an exit hole the size of an apple below his ribs.

Fargo's mount was still in motion. He wanted to holler for Mary to let go and move out of the way but couldn't with the toothpick in his mouth. Dieter was livid. He practically threw the Henry at her to free his hands so he could grab for Fargo's Colt, which was wedged under his wide leather belt.

"Look out!" Jenny screamed.

Fargo centered both .44's on the sergeant's torso. Before he could fire, Dieter's horse abruptly took several steps and blundered into the path of his. A bone-jarring jolt nearly hurled him off. Fargo's horse stayed upright but Dieter's crashed to the ground, nickering and thrashing on four legs, smashing Dieter head-first into the earth.

Dropping one of the .44's, Fargo brought his animal to a halt and reined around. Dieter was limp, either unconscious or dead. The rest of the Blues lay in spreading puddles of blood. Swinging down, he slid the toothpick into its ankle sheath, then dashed to Dieter, claimed his Colt, and twirled it into his holster.

Still holding the Henry by the barrel, Mary besieged him with questions. "Are you all right? Where have you been? What's going on?"

"Later," Fargo said, taking his rifle. "The rest of the Blues will be here any second. Are the two of you up to a long, hard ride?"

Jenny couldn't take her eyes off the blood. "Whatever you say, Mr. Fargo," she said timidly.

A chorus of shouts from the sentries and milling figures at the stable proved Fargo's prediction. He went to climb back on the horse he had used but it shied.

"Where are we going?" Mary asked. "To town?"

"It's under martial law," Fargo reminded her. "Blues will be patrolling the streets." Since the first horse wouldn't let him grab the reins, he ran to one of the others, a chestnut with a long mane and tail, and swung aboard without any problem.

"Then where?"

"There." Fargo wagged the Henry at the foothills and the towering mountains beyond. "Ladies first. I'll cover you." He worked the Henry's lever to confirm a round was in the chamber, then spurred after them. He wished he had more rifle cartridges. The Colt was all right at short range, but he needed the rifle to keep the Blues at bay, and it only contained fifteen rounds. The rest of his ammunition was packed in his saddlebags on the missing Ovaro.

Riders were barreling toward the road. One banged off several shots, but they were wide of the mark. Fargo considered dropping the culprit but opted to save his ammo for when he really needed it.

The three of them gained the pines moments later. Their horses were fresh and well-fed, and for forty-five minutes they held to a grueling pace, stopping only when the animals were flecked with sweat and beginning to flag. Fargo called the halt partway up a switchback that afforded a panoramic vista of the countryside they had covered. He scoured their back trail for a long time but saw no evidence of pursuit. "I don't get it," he commented. "They should be after us."

"Maybe they don't rate us worth the bother," Mary speculated. She had bags under her eyes from lack of sleep and was as sweaty as the horses.

"I want to go home," Jenny piped up. "I miss Samson something awful. That terrible duke wouldn't let me bring him."

"We'll go home when it's safe," Mary promised.

"When will that be?" Jenny pressed her.

Fargo reined the chestnut toward them. "When I make it safe. Right now, we climb some more."

Another thirty minutes was spent prodding the horses to the limits of their endurance. Fargo called a second halt beside a swiftly flowing stream hemmed by ample grass and saplings, and dismounted. "We'll stay here a spell," he announced.

"A long spell, I hope," Jenny said, wearily sliding down. "I'm tuckered out, Mr. Fargo. I haven't been this tired ever."

"You're doing just fine, little one," Mary said, wiping a

sleeve across her face as she, too, swung a leg over the horn and lowered to the ground. "I'm proud of how well you've handled yourself."

Fargo estimated six or seven hours of daylight were left. Wasting it would be foolish, but the Jeeters were about done in. "The two of you can take naps if you want." He removed bedrolls from their horses and spread them out near the stream. "Here you go. I'll stand watch."

Jenny was under the blankets in the blink of an eye. "Thank you, Mr. Fargo. You're a nice man."

"A very nice man," her mother emphasized, lying down beside the daughter. "If you hadn't come along I don't know what would have happened. To be honest, I feared for our lives. Otto acted strange when we parted. As if he never intended to see us again."

"He didn't," Fargo said, and imparted the conversation he had overheard.

Mary was aghast. "They were going to kill us in cold blood? Even my child?" She placed a hand on Jenny, who had closed her eyes and was drifting into dreamland. "When we reach town I'll let everyone know. Maybe that will be enough to convince the holdouts to take a stand against the madman."

"Maybe," Fargo said skeptically. Some people refused to see the truth even when it was staring them in the face. "We'll worry about that later. Try and get some rest."

"I'll try. But tired as I am, I'm so overwrought I don't know if I can." Mary lay on her side, an arm curled under her head, her other arm draped across Jenny. "I've never seen men killed before," she said softly. "It was horrible."

"Gunfights are seldom a pretty sight," Fargo agreed, and drifted over to a fifteen-foot-high knoll. From the top he had a clear view of the terrain below. There was still no sign of the Imperial Guard, which perplexed him to no end. Wolfrik wasn't the type to let the deaths of Guardsmen go unavenged. Every Blue at the estate should have been after them by now.

Seated on the top with his legs outstretched, Fargo pushed his hat back on his head and leaned back. Once the Jeeters woke up he would wait until nightfall and sneak them into town. If they picketed their horses off in the grass and snuck in on foot they could elude the Blues. Either Mrs. McGillicutty or Mrs. Keating would no doubt put Mary and Jenny up, freeing him to go after Otto Wolfrik. He wouldn't rest until the duke was dead. No matter what it took, he would put an end to the petty tyrant and the loco brainstorm that had stirred up Flathead Indians.

Twenty minutes went by. Jenny was sound asleep, but Mary tossed a lot. Twice Fargo noticed her staring at him. When, at length, she silently rose and tiptoed over, he smiled and patted the grass beside him. "Have a seat."

Mary's leg brushed his as she complied. "I tried everything I could think of to relax. Nothing worked."

"Did you count sheep?" Fargo bantered.

"No, but I did think about the two of us the other night in the pantry." Mary's shoulder and hip were so close that when she turned toward him their bodies brushed. "I wouldn't mind doing that again sometime."

"Me, either," Fargo said. He wasn't expecting her to lean over and plant a warm kiss on his mouth.

"Ever heard the saying 'there's no time like the present'?"

"Here? Now?" Fargo shook his head in amusement. "With your daughter less than thirty feet away?"

"She's exhausted. She wouldn't wake up if the world came to an end." Mary scooted a yard lower down the opposite side of the knoll, and crooked a finger. "We could do it here where she couldn't see, and you could still keep an eye on her. We'd have to be discreet about it."

"You're serious?" Fargo asked. He shouldn't have been surprised. Once some women tasted intimacy they continually craved more. Some of the primmest, most strait-laced females he'd ever met had turned into boiling cauldrons of lust once they unleashed their pent-up desires. He hadn't imagined Mary as the sort, but women were always full of pleasant contradictions.

"I can't think of a better way to relax, can you?" Mary put a hand on his leg and ran her fingers from his ankle to just above his knee, inside his thigh.

Fargo's manhood twitched and his throat constricted. He scoured the country below, glanced at Jenny, then slowly slid down until he was level with Mary. "You're a bundle of surprises, you know that?"

"What's the harm if we don't wake Jenny?" Mary kissed him again, intensely, her soft tongue caressing his teeth and gums. Closing her eyes, she opened her arms wide and melted into him.

Fargo kept his eyes open. It wouldn't do to let down his guard, not when the Blues still might show up. But if they did, he was confident he'd spot them from a long way off and have plenty of time to rouse the girl and light a shuck.

Mary drew back, her eyelids hooded with desire. "It's too bad you're not the marrying kind or I'd stake a claim. You do things to me . . ." Her fingers roamed over his chest, her mouth nibbled at his throat.

"I could say the same," Fargo whispered, rolling her onto her back. His pole was stiffening, a bulge forming in his pants. He rose up on his hands high enough to check on Jenny, who slumbered peacefully, then gripped Mary by the waist and ground against her. "See what I mean?"

Giggling, Mary dipped a hand and stroked him.

A ball of heat radiated outward from Fargo's center. He sucked on her velvet tongue while kneading her right breast. Under his palm the nipple hardened and she squirmed deliciously.

Mary entwined her fingers behind his neck. Her left leg slid up and down his thigh, provoking tiny tingles. "I'm so relaxed I could melt," she quipped after they broke their kiss long enough to catch a breath.

"I'll bet you could." Fargo licked and flicked her earlobes, which were especially sensitive, and lathered the soft junction of her neck and right shoulder. Her hands shifted to his upper arms, molding his biceps and triceps, while her knee slowly rose toward his ever-swelling bulge. He slipped his arms down around her buttocks and cupped them, squeezing them through her dress.

Panting, Mary shifted to grant him access to her nether charms. Their next kiss was volcanic, their lips seamless, their tongues dancing in satiny abandon.

Fargo would have liked nothing better than to strip her and feast on her naked delights, but Mary had been right about the need to stay dressed. He checked on Jenny again, then roved a hand between Mary's smooth thighs. Her dress clung to his fingers as he caressed her. He deliberately resisted touching her slit. That could wait a bit, until she was burning with need.

In nearby trees jays squawked and squirrels chattered, signs they were in no immediate danger. If the birds and animals were to suddenly fall silent, then there would be cause for alarm.

Hiking her dress so he could slip his hand further underneath, Fargo savored the cushiony softness of her skin. He stroked her inner thighs, moving higher by gradual degrees to tantalize her, as she wriggled and gasped, raining kisses on his forehead, his cheeks, his chin.

"Ohhhhh, I like that," Mary whispered.

Fargo could tell. She liked it even more when his finger pried her undergarments apart and touched her moist opening. At the contact she arched her spine, her mouth wide in a soundless moan. Wetness dampened his fingertip as he stroked from her bush to her buttocks. She was dripping, and oh so hot. Inserting his fingertip, he lightly played with her swollen knob.

Mary bit him. She sank her teeth into his shoulder and bit down hard, either to stifle another moan or simply out of raw passion.

Fargo winced but continued to stroke her. Ever so slowly he delved his forefinger into her molten tunnel, feeling her inner walls ripple and contract. Her bottom came up off the ground and bucked against him, seeking to drive him deeper, seeking to sink him as far as his finger could go.

Fargo's manhood throbbed for release, but he held off. He

began to pump his finger in and out, over and over again, increasing her craving. She kissed his face, his neck, and thrust her hips against him in wanton fever. Yet not once did she make a sound. Whenever the urge came over her, she tossed her head back, her lips clamped tight, her throat quivering.

Again Fargo checked on the child. He also twisted to gaze down the mountain. Sparrows were chirping in the brush and somewhere a chipmunk was making a racket all out of proportion to its diminutive size.

Satisfied all was well, Fargo spread her legs wider and inserted a second finger. Mary shot up off the grass, clinging fast, her breaths heavy in his ear.

"Yessss. Oh, yesssssss!"

Fargo felt her shift, felt her fingers tug at his pants. In a few moments his pole jutted free and her hand wrapped around him. He began to breath heavily himself. She delicately traced a nail from the bottom to the tip, then swirled her finger around and round, down to the bottom again.

"Do it soon. Please," Mary said.

Pulling her dress higher, Fargo knelt between her thighs and guided himself to her womanhood. She trembled when he rubbed his member along her slit, trembled even more as he started to sheathe his pulsing sword in her yielding scabbard. He fed himself to her slowly, and when he was all the way in he held still.

Mary gripped his wrist, her eyes shimmering with desire. "Now. Please."

Rocking back on his knees, Fargo suddenly spiked up into her. Mary's eyes flared wide. He rocked again, and again, pacing himself, as her legs wrapped tight and her ankles locked behind his back. They were joined, their two bodies one, her movements synchronized with his, just as they had been that night in the pantry.

They barely made any noise. The grass muffled whatever sounds their clothes didn't. Except for their heavy breathing, the tranquility of the afternoon was undisturbed. No one ten feet away could have known what they were up to. Certainly

Jenny couldn't hear, and that was all that mattered to Fargo. He went faster, Mary matching his tempo.

"Ah! I'm almost there!"

Her whisper brought Fargo close to the brink. He gritted his teeth to stave the explosion off for as long as possible. Was it another minute or was it three when Mary clutched him and bit her own lip as her body writhed in the ecstasy of total release. She gushed like a geyser, drenching him.

"I'm coming!"

So did Fargo, in an eruption that blurred the world. Fueled by raw pleasure he became a living piston. Pumping, always pumping, his entire body vibrant, he attained the pinnacle he was striving for. He was conscious of Mary and himself, and that was all. Not until he was totally spent did he coast to a stop and sink down on her, perspiring and breathless.

"Thank you," Mary panted.

Fargo lay there catching his breath, his cheek buoyed by her heaving breasts, his head rising and falling to the rhythm of her heavy breathing. He could hear her heart fluttering like a butterfly's wings. Sleep nipped at him and he nearly succumbed. As he was about to go under he thought of Duke Wolfrik and the Blues and he jerked his head up to keep from falling asleep.

Wisps of hair hung over Mary's face. Eyes closed, a smile of contentment curling her flawless face, she sighed happily.

Mentally flogging himself to sit up, Fargo verified Jenny hadn't stirred. He rolled off Mary and pulled the hem of her dress down to her knees. He would very much like to lie there for the rest of the day, but circumstances dictated differently. Putting his hands flat, he slowly rose and stretched.

Mary was dozing off, her arms across her waist, a portrait of loveliness.

Fargo decided to have a look around. Grasping the Henry, he unfurled, then stood there admiring her a while. She was sound asleep when he finally turned to scout the area. But he only took two steps.

Twenty feet away were a dozen Flathead in full war paint.

Arrayed in a semicircle, they were armed with bows, lances, and war clubs. At their center was Iron Fist, head and shoulders above the rest, his lance longer and thicker than any other. Most of the warriors were grinning, Iron Fist the widest of all.

Taken completely off guard for one of the few times in his entire life, Fargo was riveted in astonishment. He glanced at Mary, who was lightly snoring, then thought to hitch up his pants and adjust his gunbelt.

"We meet again," Iron Fist said.

"We meet again," Fargo responded, at a loss for anything else to say.

Iron Fist bobbed his chin at Mary. "Pretty woman you have."

"Very pretty," Fargo agreed.

"We watch you some while."

"I was afraid of that." Judging by their grins Fargo guessed they had seen quite a lot. The Flatheads thought it was humorous, but he didn't share the sentiment. Making love was something he preferred to do in private. His cheeks began to burn and he swore under his breath.

"This day I give you Flathead name," Iron Fist declared. "We call you Longhorn Bull. How that be?" He translated for the benefit of his companions and to a man they burst out laughing.

Fargo joined in despite himself. "I like it," he admitted. "You honor me greatly."

"I see buffalo like you once," Iron Fist remarked, again translating for his friends.

Their new round of mirth roused Mary, who sat up in confusion, saw the warriors, and leaped erect as if she had been seated on hot coals. "Savages! Run for your life!" Belatedly, she realized they were laughing and stopped backing away. "What in the world? Do you know them, Skye? What is this?"

Fargo made to explain, but Iron Fist answered first.

"Pretty woman, we give you Flathead name too. We call you Deepest Cave. How that be?"

"Deepest Cave?" Mary asked, her confusion compounded.

Her forehead knit and she looked at Fargo, then at the mound, then at the warriors again. "Oh my God! Please tell me that doesn't mean what I think it means."

"Afraid so," Fargo said, and laughed anew when Mary placed a hand over her mouth and staggered as if she were about to faint.

"You think this is *funny*?" Indignation brought Mary to a halt with her fists clenched. "They saw us doing—!" She couldn't bring herself to complete the statement so she simply screeched, *"They saw us!"*

Fargo was sorry, truly sorry. "Try to stay clam. They're Flatheads. They're friendly. No real harm was done."

"No harm?" Mary was flabbergasted. "The next time, invite the whole Flathead nation, why don't you? Hell, invite everyone in town, too. I'm sure they'd all enjoy the show!"

"I didn't mean—" Fargo began, but she wasn't listening. She was hurrying to Jenny, who had sat up and was rubbing her eyes.

"Why Deepest Cave mad?" Iron Fist inquired, coming forward.

"She's a woman, that's her job."

Iron Fist grunted, then pivoted and waved an arm. Out of the pines came more warriors, among them Running Badger, leading the Ovaro.

"I wondered where he got to," Fargo said.

"Running Badger see us from hill. Come get us," Iron Fist explained. "When we reach hill, you gone. So we track you."

"Why'd he take my horse?" Fargo asked.

"Him afraid maybe bluecoats come."

So there it was. Running Badger had thought a patrol might happen by. Fargo accepted the stallion's reins and patted its neck. Now he had all the ammo he needed. But he wouldn't be going after the duke alone.

"Time has come," Iron Fist said solemnly, placing a hand on Fargo's shoulder. "Time we kill Hairless Snake."

12

Whatever else might be said about Duke Otto Wolfrik, he was no fool. He had sent for the rest of his Imperial Guard, as Skye Fargo learned when he and six dozen Flatheads arrived on the hilltop overlooking the estate an hour after sunset. Over thirty Blues were bustling about below, transforming the grounds into a military encampment. Perimeter fires were ablaze. Guardsmen with rifles were posted on the roofs of the mansion, barracks, and stable. Many more lined a freshly dug trench about five feet deep, that ran from the mansion.

That wasn't all.

In the fading light Fargo spied a mortar at each end of the trench. Only two, but their range and destructive force would rout the Flatheads if the duke were allowed to bring them to bear. "See those metal tubes?" he asked Iron Fist, pointing.

"What they be?" the Flathead said.

"Ever seen a canon?"

Iron Fist scowled. "At Missouri River fort. Big gun. Big noise. Make hole like cave. These do same?"

"Not quite," Fargo said. "But they can blow a man or a horse to bits if they hit dead on. They can reach us from there if Wolfrik spots us." He hunkered and the Flathead did the same. "We can't let the Blues use them. Pick a dozen or more of your best archers. When the attack begins, have them put enough arrows into the soldiers manning the tubes to turn them into porcupines."

"We do," Iron Fist said.

"As for the riflemen on the roofs, have the bowmen shoot fire arrows to drive them off," Fargo proposed. "The Blues in the trench will be harder to get to but you have enough warriors to beat them if—" He stopped. Three figures had appeared, walking along the excavation. One was Duke Otto Wolfrik. The second was Sergeant Dieter, limping badly. The third was a frail, elderly Flathead, who shambled along stooped over, his wrists bound behind his back.

"Gray Wolf!" Iron Fist exclaimed, rising.

Other warriors had spotted the chief. Word spread like a prairie fire and to a man they thronged to the hill's rim, jeopardizing their lives in their concern for their leader.

"Get down!" Fargo cautioned, but he might as well have saved his breath. He saw Wolfrik and Dieter stop beside a six-foot pole imbedded in the ground. The sergeant barked at a pair of Blues, who climbed out and proceeded to tie Gray Wolf to the pole.

Iron Fist nudged Fargo. "Why they do that?"

"It's insurance." Fargo didn't like how the warriors were muttering and hefting their weapons. They were making too much noise and would give themselves away if they kept it up.

"I not understand."

"It's Hairless Snake's way of warning you off. If you attack, his men will gun Gray Wolf down before you can reach him." Fargo straightened. One of the Flatheads was gesturing and raising his voice dangerously loud. "Tell the rest. And have them keep quiet while you're at it."

Iron Fist whispered to the man next to him, who relayed the message on down the line. One by one the Flatheads fell silent, their expressions masks of resentment.

Fargo scratched his chin. "So long as the duke has Gray Wolf we can't do a thing." The solution was obvious. "So we'll pull him out before we hit them."

"Pull out how?"

Tilting his head back, Fargo surveyed the stars. "Hairless Snake has to let his men sleep sometime. We'll wait until the middle of the night. Then I'll go in and cut Gray Wolf loose."

"You not go alone," Iron Fist said.

Fargo would rather do it himself; there was less chance of

being caught. But arguing would be fruitless. Instead, he drew Iron Fist to one side and for the next hour and a half they went over how to wage battle against the Imperial Guard. Iron Fist was in favor of a frontal attack, but Fargo convinced him a great many warriors would needlessly die. Locating a stick, he sketched the buildings in the dirt and suggested where and how the Flatheads should strike to best advantage.

Iron Fist agreed to every suggestion. At the end he clapped Fargo on the back and thanked him for his help.

"Thank me again if we win." Fargo stood and walked past huddled knots of warriors to where Mary and Jenny Jeeter were seated on a blanket, Jenny's head in her mother's lap. "Still mad at me?" he asked. Mary hadn't spoken ten words to him since the incident at the knoll.

"I suppose not," she said begrudgingly.

"I'm not mad," Jenny said, eyeing the Flatheads as if in fear of being scalped. "I'm scared."

"They won't hurt you. They're on our side." Fargo squatted. "I've had a talk with Iron Fist. If something should happen to me he's agreed to personally escort you to town."

"What if Otto wins?" Mary asked. "What if he routs the Indians and you take a bullet. Where does that leave us?"

Fargo mulled the choices they had. "Sneak into town. Ask one of your friends for enough food and water to last a month, then head south. The first river you come to, go east. Eventually you'll come to a settlement."

"Just the two of us? Alone? In all those endless miles of prairie?"

"Ask a man you trust to go along. Luke Barstow is dependable." In Fargo's opinion, any man who would take the beating Barstow had to spare a little girl from being hurt had to be decent at heart.

Mary touched his arm. "I'll do it. But if I had my druthers it would be you. So be careful. Please."

"Always."

Iron Fist was roving among the Flatheads, explaining what would be required of them later. Some were honing knives.

Some were sharpening arrow points, or testing sinew bow strings. A few were softly chanting. Several smiled at Fargo as he walked back to his vantage point and hunkered.

Little movement was evident below. Occasionally a Blue would feed logs to a perimeter fire, but for the most part they were waiting and watching. Fargo saw Duke Wolfrik and Sergeant Dieter go into the mansion.

Gray Wolf was in a bad way. His body sagged, his head was bent low. Were it not for the rope binding him to the pole he would have pitched onto his face.

Fargo considered trying to get some sleep and dismissed the idea. He was too tense, too on edge. Besides, if he did manage to doze off for a few hours he might wake up sluggish, his reflexes dulled, and he needed to be at his best when the time came to put his plan into effect.

Some of the Flatheads, though, had no such qualms, and presently a third of the warriors were stretched out on the ground, napping. Iron Fist wasn't one of them. Coming over, he squatted, his forearms across his knees. "I tell all. They be ready."

"No one objected?" Fargo asked. Since he was white, he'd assumed a few wouldn't trust him enough to go along with his plan.

Iron Fist grasped as much. "We want our chief. Your way good way. Few die. So we do your way."

"There are no guarantees," Fargo stressed. Not in war. Not when random chance was the deciding element. All it would take was for an observant Blue to spot them before they freed Gray Wolf and it would all fall apart. "Don't blame me if things go wrong."

"We not blame you. We blame bluecoats. We blame Hairless Snake." Iron Fist glowered. "He must die. All warriors agree. Warrior who see him, kill him."

"Not if I get a crack at him first," Fargo said.

"What about later?" Iron Fist asked. "What army do?"

"After it's over I'll go to the nearest post and tell the commanding officer what happened," Fargo said. "They know me.

They'll believe me. A report will be sent to Washington clearing you of blame. No one will hold it against you."

"Good. We not want this fight. We not want all whites hate us."

A light came on in one of the upper rooms, bathing the window in a rosy glow. The curtains were open, and Fargo saw Duke Otto Wolfrik cross the room and light several candles in long-stemmed holders. Above them, attached to the wall, was a silver cross. Wolfrik made the sign of the cross, then dropped onto his knees and clasped his hands.

"What him do?" Iron Fist inquired.

Fargo could scarcely credit his eyes. "He's praying. Calling on the white god to help him, would be my guess." Never in a million years would he have thought the duke was religious, but he had to remember Wolfrik was from the Old Country, and old habits were hard to let go of.

"No god save him now," Iron Fist vowed.

Wolfrik didn't stay long. Within a few minutes he had risen, blown out the candles, and left.

Over the next several hours little else occurred. Corporal Treffen made a couple of trips to the stable. Sergeant Dieter came from the house once to walk along the trench. Afterward, half the Blues curled up on the ground to get some rest. On his way back to the house Dieter looked straight at the hill but gave no indication of having cause for alarm.

"Soon now, eh?" Iron Fist said.

"Soon," Fargo agreed. He gave it another hour to ensure the soldiers who had turned in were asleep and those keeping watch would be drowsy and unfocused. Then he rose. "Tell the rest it's time. Remind them they must not make any noise. Your chief's life depends on it."

Eager to begin, Iron Fist hustled off, whispering excitedly, rousing his fellow Flatheads. Fargo glanced toward the blankets. Jenny was asleep. Mary was staring at him, and smiled encouragement.

The warriors formed into groups, depending on the part they were to play in the overall strategy. First to sneak down the slope were the archers; it was crucial they be in position before anyone else. Next to go were a dozen warriors picked to create a diversion Fargo hoped would distract the Blues long enough for Iron Fist and him to cut Gray Wolf loose and whisk the chief out of there.

"Our turn," the tall warrior said.

Together, they stalked down through the pines until they were close to the ring of light cast by the perimeter fires. Fargo leaned the Henry against a trunk and palmed his Colt. Iron Fist did likewise with his spear, drawing a bone-handled knife instead.

The fires were spaced approximately twenty yards apart. Fargo intended to slip past them by crawling midway between the nearest pair. A risky proposition, since it was open ground. Nodding at Iron Fist, he crouched and slowly advanced until he was at the edge of the undergrowth. The next move was up to the dozen warriors he had sent to the east, toward the stable.

Within a minute a sharp whinny came from the corral beside it. The horses began milling about and soon were nickering nonstop. The timely distraction was no coincidence; Flatheads hidden in trees pelted the animals with small rocks.

Fargo watched the Guardsmen in the trench. Their heads and upper torsos were visible, and to a man they turned toward the corral, puzzled by the commotion. So did the riflemen on the roofs.

Fargo gestured at Iron Fist and slid from the tall weeds on his belly. The horses were making quite a racket, squealing every time a stone struck them, and now Corporal Treffen climbed out of the trench and jogged toward the corral, several Blues accompanying him, their sabers rattling.

Fargo went faster. Soon he was well past the fires and mired in shadow. None of the Blues in the trench were paying any attention to their prisoner. He saw a head poke above the mansion but even the rifleman was gazing toward the horses. A second later Iron Fist passed him, crawling swiftly, recklessly. Fargo whispered to slow down, but the tall warrior ignored him.

Another horse squealed in pain. Most of the Blues in the trench moved toward the end nearest the stable to better see what was going on.

Fargo tried to catch up to his Flathead ally, but Iron Fist had taken off like a bat out of hell. A face appeared at a ground-floor mansion window, lingered a bit, and then withdrew. He couldn't tell if it had been the duke or someone else, and he prayed whoever it was hadn't seen them.

Corporal Treffen was near the corral now, peering intently toward the forest. Evidently he suspected the source of the disturbance, as his men trained their rifles on the vegetation.

Iron Fist glanced back as if annoyed at how slow Fargo was going. In another five yards he would reach the pole.

All the Blues were watching Corporal Treffen, who barked an order and advanced toward the pines, the Guardsmen with him formed a skirmish line.

Fargo had six feet to go when Iron Fist began slicing at the ropes binding Gray Wolf's ankles. The chief never stirred. He appeared to be unconscious. Iron Fist made short shrift of the loops and rose to cut those securing Gray Wolf's wrists.

Another horse whinnied, and Corporal Treffen bawled in Transian. He had figured out that rocks were being thrown. Shouldering his rifle, he cut loose, firing at random into the trees. His men followed his lead and began firing as well.

The Flatheads didn't return fire. They had been instructed to wait for a signal from Iron Fist, who was slicing in a fury at the last of the ropes. They parted, and Gray Wolf toppled, right into Iron Fist's arms.

Fargo reached them and rose. All the Guardsmen in the trench were riveted on Corporal Treffen, but that could change at any second. Iron Fist headed north and he followed, backpedaling. Constantly glancing from the trench to the roofs to the stable, he began to think they might make it when a yell from the front of the mansion shattered the illusion.

The gunfire had brought Duke Wolfrik and Sergeant Dieter to the front porch, and it was the latter who pointed at them and bellowed at the top of his lungs, clutching his revolver.

Some of the Blues in the trench swung around. On the roof of the mansion a Guardsman swiveled and took hasty aim.

Fargo and Iron Fist were caught flatfooted. "Do it now!" Fargo shouted at the Flathead, and Iron Fist threw back his head and gave voice to a fierce war whoop.

Out of the darkness streaked a flight of arrows. Corporal Treffen and men were caught by surprise. The Flathead arrows found their targets, and Treffen and his men died in their tracks. At the same instant a dozen warriors burst from the undergrowth, racing toward the stable. Soldiers in the trench commenced firing, some at Fargo and Iron Fist, some at the onrushing Flatheads.

The battle had been joined.

Fargo banged off two swift shots and saw a Guardsman topple. He sprang to help Iron Fist as fire arrows arced out of the ether, arrows the Flatheads had wrapped in hide and touched to the perimeter fires. Several stuck in the barracks roof, others landed with loud thuds on the mansion. The rest streaked at the Blues in the trench. One man took a shaft high in the shoulder, another low in the chest. Both screamed, the first man frantically swatting at the flames so his uniform wouldn't catch ablaze.

A revolver boomed out front. Fargo heard a slug whiz past his ear and returned fire, shooting twice at Sergeant Dieter and the duke, both of whom dived flat.

Out of the forest poured another twenty screeching, whooping Flatheads. As they had been instructed, they charged the trench. They had the most difficult chore of all, to keep the Blues there occupied for a while without being mowed down.

Riflemen on the roofs opened fire, dropping a few of the charging Flatheads. Not enough to break the charge, and not enough to prevent the warriors from unleashing a cloud of arrows and lances that rained on the trench by the dozens. Added to it were more shafts fired by the archers in the trees, who had turned their attention to the same targets. Just as Fargo had told them to do. Over a third of the Blues were transfixed. Those who weren't were smart and had ducked for cover.

In another ten yards Fargo and Iron Fist would reach the hill.

Gray Wolf moaned and lifted his head. The old chief's face was battered and discolored, and his right hand was caked with dried blood from the finger that had been hacked off. Terribly thin from a lack of food, he tried to move of his own accord, but he was much too weak.

The Blues in the trench fired a ragged volley, felling the foremost Flatheads. The charge slowed but was reinforced within seconds by another wave of warriors who streamed around the west end of the mansion.

A Blue on the roof took an arrow through the throat. Shoving onto his knees, he grabbed the feathered end and mindlessly plucked it. Along with the shaft gushed a gallon of scarlet, pouring over his chest. Swaying, he rose but couldn't keep his footing and toppled over the edge, screaming all the way to the ground.

"Not far!" Iron Fist cried.

Fargo firmed his hold. They passed the perimeter fires and were caught in the glare. Suddenly the earth around them spewed dirt geysers. Duke Wolfrik and Sergeant Dieter were trying to bring them down. Twisting, Fargo extended his Colt and fired, but he was barreling along flat-out and burdened by supporting Gray Wolf. Small wonder he missed.

Dieter pushed up onto his knees, adopted a two-handed grip, and took precise aim.

Fargo snapped the Colt up. But just then another flight of fire arrows embedded themselves in the porch a few feet from the sergeant and the duke. They did what any sane person would do and scrambled closer to the wall where they were less likely to be hit.

A series of volleys from the trench brought most of the Flatheads to a halt. The Guardsmen were working their rifles as rapidly as they could to preserve their lives. A distinct *crump* from the west end preceded the spectacular flight of a rocket that spewed writhing coils of smoke and overshot the Flatheads, detonating among a cluster of pines halfway up the hill.

The third and last large wave of Flatheads, who had circled to come up on the trench from the rear, now rose up out of the grass and were in among the startled Imperial Guard in no time.

Over at the stable another savage conflict was in progress. The duke had posted men inside to protect the horses and they were locked in a life-or-death struggle with warriors assigned to stampede the stock.

A deafening explosion rocked the air. A grenade had been thrown by a Blue in the trench in a last, desperate bid to drive the Flatheads off. Five warriors were left convulsing and pumping blood, but the rest were undeterred.

Fargo and Iron Fist were almost to the brush. He let go, hollering, "You're on your own!" and spun. Iron Fist could take care of the chief. He had something more important to do.

A whirlwind of raw violence gripped the estate. Guns crackled like fireworks. Few arrows were flying because the combat was primarily man-to-man. Heated, frenzied struggles were taking place everywhere, punctuated by shrieks and curses.

Most of the rooftop riflemen had been slain by bowmen, and the Guardsmen at the stable had been slain to the last soldier. Only the troops in the trench were offering resistance and they were greatly outnumbered.

Fargo ran toward where he had last seen Duke Wolfrik and Sergeant Dieter. Neither were there, but the front door was partly ajar. Slowing, he peeked past the jamb and saw the butler, Velga, running toward him armed with a revolver. Throwing the door wide, he cried out, "Drop your gun!"

Velga had other ideas. Leveling the big .44, he snapped off a hasty shot that ripped into the jamb. Chips flew every which way.

Fargo stroked the Colt. At the blast the butler was hurled back and crashed against a sculpture. Sidling inside, Fargo strained his ears but heard nothing to indicate where Wolfrik and Dieter had gone. He came to the sitting room and glanced in. It appeared to be empty so he moved on.

Upstairs, footsteps pounded. The men he was after or another servant? Fargo wondered, halting. A new sound, directly behind him, brought him around in a crouch, goosebumps breaking out all over his flesh. It was the unmistakable rattle of one of the most dangerous serpents on the continent.

Duke Otto Wolfrik had a rattler in each hand. Face aglow with sadistic glee, he cackled and tossed them underhand. The snakes whipped end over end, their mouths agape, venom dripping from their curved fangs.

Only two and a half yards separated Fargo from the duke. He had no time to leap aside, no chance to duck. In a blur he fanned the Colt twice, shooting by pure instinct, just as he often did when practicing with bottles and sticks tossed into the air. With each shot the head of a snake was obliterated.

Snarling like a beast at bay, Duke Otto Wolfrik leaped into the sitting room and slammed the door shut, shaking the entire wall.

Fargo sidled toward it. Fingers flying, he replaced spent cartridges. He gave the cylinder a spin, thumbed back the hammer, and gripped the latch. A metallic click from within prompted him to spring back just as a .44 cracked three times and three holes dotted the panel.

"Come get me, American!" Wolfrik shrieked. "I defy you to try!"

Fargo kicked at the latch and the door swung in. Again the .44 discharged, the slug thumping into the corridor wall. Furtive movement warned Fargo the duke was changing position. Removing his hat, he dropped it on the floor, then eased forward.

"What's the matter, American?" Duke Wolfrik baited him. "Are you afraid? If not, show yourself! I am waiting!" The Beaumont-Adams belched lead that tore into the wood an inch from Fargo's cheek.

By Fargo's count the duke only had one cartridge left. Coiling, he threw himself into the sitting room, rolling as he landed to make himself harder to hit. The .44 thundered, the bullet tearing into floorboards a hand's width from his head. Pushing erect, Fargo saw Wolfrik cast the revolver down and grab a jar from the mantle. Inside was the same large rattler the duke had been holding the first time Fargo saw him.

"Die, damn you!" Wolfrik railed, raising the jar overhead to throw it.

"Not today," Fargo said, firing as he spoke, one shot into the center of the jar.

The glass shattered, coming apart in Duke Wolfrik hands. Out tumbled the huge rattlesnake, wounded, incensed, and biting right and left. The duke screamed and attempted to spring to safety but the snake landed across his neck and shoulders. In a panic he struck at it with his fists and the viper bit him in the throat. Three, four, five times the fangs sank home.

"No!" Wolfrik wailed. Tearing the reptile off, he threw it aside and moved toward the hall, his legs wobbling. "Not like this!" he declared. "It can't end like this!"

Fargo followed.

The duke made it to the hall and turned toward the entrance but only went a few steps when his legs buckled. Nails scraping the wall as he sank down, he whimpered, sounding a lot like Samson that day in the forest. The snake's fangs had pierced a major artery and the venom was working swiftly.

Saying nothing, Fargo awaited the outcome.

"You!" Wolfrik said, his eyes dilated with fear. "I command you to help me! Suck the venom out and I still have a chance."

"Like I told you before," Fargo said, reclaiming his hat, "don't hold your breath." He stepped over the duke's legs.

"Stop!" Wolfrik croaked. "Didn't you hear me! I command you! I, Duke Otto Wolfrik of the imperial House of Wolfrik order you to—"

Strangled gurgling fell on Fargo's ears but he didn't look back until he reached the front door. The duke was on his back, flopping about like a fish out of water, each ragged breath more and more labored. As Fargo looked on, Wolfrik's chest stopped heaving and the duke was still.

Outside the battle was winding down. The mansion, the barracks, and the stable were on fire. Bodies littered the ground, laying in heaps around the trench where the fighting had been fiercest. Among them was that of Sergeant Dieter, a long, thick lance protruding from his chest.

Iron Fist, Running Badger, and other warriors spotted Fargo and hurried over to the porch Iron Fist shaking the bloody knife he held. "Hairless Snake?"

"Dead," Fargo said.

The tall warrior translated and those with him whooped in glee. Fargo then watched them sprint toward the last pocket of resistance. He turned and trudged up the hill, retrieving the Henry along the way. The Jeeters were waiting at the top.

"You're alive!" Mary rejoiced, throwing her arms around him.

"No thanks to Wolfrik," Fargo said, breathing deep of her perfume. "I can take you back to town now if you'd like." He wanted to spare the little girl the sight of the Blues being scalped, or worse.

"What will happen to the folks in town?" Jenny asked.

A good question. With the duke gone, the town would shrivel and die. "I'll guide them to the nearest settlement," Fargo proposed. "They can decide what they want to do from there."

Mary pecked his chin. "Do we have to pack up and leave right away?"

Fargo smiled. He could use a hot bath, enough food to gag a bear, and a couple days in bed. Not necessarily alone. "There's no rush. We can take our time."

"I was hoping you would say that," Mary Jeeter said, and winked.

LOOKING FORWARD!

**The following is the opening
section from the next novel in the exciting
Trailsman series from Signet:**

**THE TRAILSMAN #236
DENVER CITY GOLD**

*Colorado Territory, 1859—When greed sets off a
gold-fever epidemic, and lead poisoning is a lethal
symptom—only the Trailsman can cure what ails.*

The sharp crack of the bullwhip drowned out the buzz of the black flies bedeviling Skye Fargo. The Trailsman swatted at the annoying bugs but knew it would do no good. Ever since the freight wagons had reached the uneven plains of eastern Colorado, the bugs had been swarming around his face, around his Ovaro, and around the long team of mules struggling to pull the heavily laden wagons bound for Denver City.

Fargo turned and scanned the terrain, hunting for level expanses to make the going easier for the freighters. Their mules were tuckered out from struggling over the rolling hills. Fargo had argued with Clem Parson before they left, but the wagonmaster had been adamant. He wanted Fargo to scout a shorter route and to hell with what that land west of Kansas City looked like, as long as they reached Denver City ahead of two competing freighters. Parson hoped to win lucrative contracts to supply the boom town merchants with not only staple goods but the far more profitable luxury items.

In the back of the wagon Parson expertly drove, clanked and clattered a heavy iron Ramage press. The owner of the *Rocky Mountain News* had lost his printing press in a fire, and when Parson delivered this one, Bill Byers would again be able to put his newspaper into every eager Denverite's hand. Clem Parson figured the publicity gained would aid his cause since Byers was a generous man and helped anyone willing to see Denver grow.

"There are gullies ahead," Fargo called to Parson. The grizzled mule skinner rocked back, ready to crack his whip again, but hearing Fargo's warning he relaxed and put the whip back into its holder at his side.

"Where do we head, then?"

Fargo knew how important it was to Parson to arrive before his competition, but bulling on and getting bogged down in the maze of ravines with such heavily laden wagons would slow them more than taking a rest.

"Stay here. I'll scout ahead and be back before sundown."

"Sundown? Hell, Fargo, that's two hours off!" Parson held up his hand to shield the sun and estimate how much travel time he would lose.

"Give the mules a rest now and you'll get twice the work out of them tomorrow," Fargo promised.

"I suppose," Parson said with ill grace. He stood in the driver's box and waved to the four wagons behind his to circle for the night.

"Don't worry so much, Clem. I'll get you to Denver within the week."

"Not if we spend all our time lollygaggin' around a campfire," groused Parson with mock vexation. "Do what you can, Fargo. You done all right up till now, so I don't reckon you'll abandon us out here on the plains."

"You can see the Rockies," Fargo said. "That's where we're heading. It's just a matter of finding the best route."

"Then get to it, man, get to it!" Parson grabbed his twenty-foot-long bullwhip and gave it a resounding crack in Fargo's direction. Fargo's Ovaro reared, pawed at the hot, still Colorado air, then took off at a trot in the direction of the troublesome ravines.

Fargo took every chance he could to ride along the top of the ridges crisscrossing the area so he could pick a path that would afford Parson and his wagons the easiest travel. After an hour of scouting, he thought he had found the best route—and one that would get the wagon train to Denver two days ahead of an already ambitious schedule. As he turned to retrace the route he had chosen, he reined back and stared at the bottom of a rocky-bottom wash. He had been so intent on finding a route for the freighters he had missed a set of fresh tracks.

Fargo frowned, trying to figure out why anyone would follow the wash as the wagon obviously had. He dismounted and walked along the tracks. As he studied the ground more closely, he became more curious. Not only had a wagon drawn by six oxen come along, so had no fewer than three horses, all shod. From the way the fitful wind had slightly rounded the wagon tracks but not the hoofprints, he guessed the riders were at least an hour behind the wagon.

In this empty land, he knew no reason riders would follow a wagon unless they were scouts returning to report on their survey. But three? More? What single wagon needed so many scouts?

Fargo found himself torn between returning directly to where Parson and his men camped, and investigating this mystery. There was still an hour of sunlight left. If he galloped his sturdy pinto, the freighters might get another fifteen or twenty minutes of travel in today. Then he pushed that notion from his head. Parson would have already unhitched the teams and corralled the mules inside the ring of wagons. It would take more than fifteen minutes to get them hitched up again. Why risk travelling after sunset?

Not sure what worried him, Fargo mounted and rode along the trail left by the wagon. The wagon had pulled out of the ravine and struggled across the prairie less than a mile from where Fargo first had come across the tracks. What puzzled him now was how the horses had vanished. Their riders had abandoned their pursuit of the wagon on some rocky ground.

Fargo knew he ought to turn around and report to Clem Parson. The freighter was a good employer, a generous man in spite of his gruffness, and was due a timely report on the result of Fargo's scouting. Parson deserved it, but something gnawed away at Fargo until he couldn't stand it any longer. He put his heels to the Ovaro's flanks and picked up the pace, chasing after the lone wagon.

As the red sun dipped behind the Rockies, showing the jagged peaks in the far distance clearly now, Fargo spotted the wagon. He reined back and watched as three dim figures bustled about the rear of the Conestoga. They weren't pitching camp. They were too engaged pointing at the rear of the wagon and arguing with each other.

Fargo made no effort to hide his approach. He rode boldly and slowly so as not to spook the three. As he neared the wagon with its oxen team restlessly stirring in poorly maintained yokes, he saw two men in their twenties arguing while a woman somewhere between them in age stood by and stared at the wagon, as if this might miraculously fix it.

"Howdy," called Fargo, startling the trio. "See you've got a busted wheel. Anything I can do to help?"

"Who're you?" cried the younger of the men, reaching into the back of the wagon and pulling out a shotgun.

"Don't go pointing that at anyone you don't mean to shoot," Fargo said, irritated. "If you don't want my help, say so."

"I'm sorry, mister," the woman said, stepping out of the shadows that had partially hidden her face from Fargo's view. He caught his breath and knew why the man was so quick with the shotgun. If he had a woman as lovely as this one, he'd be protective of her, too.

The woman was small, hardly topping five feet tall, but her feminine figure was full and her face was a vision of angelic loveliness. She brushed back a strand of dusty brown hair and looked at him with ginger-colored eyes that were both frank and inviting.

"We might need some help. Don't you agree, Zeb? Ben?"

Fargo saw the young man with the shotgun wince at the implied criticism of the armed greeting and pegged him to be Zeb. Ben was no more inclined toward friendliness than Zeb. Looking hard at them, Fargo thought they might be brothers.

"I'm Susanna Grafton," the woman said, coming over to him. He tipped his hat to her, then reached down and shook her hand when she thrust it out like a man might. As he introduced himself, he couldn't help noticing her shiny gold wedding ring as she impulsively brushed her hair away from her sparkling eyes.

Susanna stepped back and stared at the two men. Fargo wondered which of them was her husband and which was her brother-in-law. If he had to pick, the less impulsive Ben must be Mr. Grafton.

"Well, Mr. Grafton," Fargo said, dismounting, "let's see what the problem is."

"I can tell you," spoke up Zeb. "We busted the damned wheel!"

"Zeb! Watch your language!" snapped Susanna. This stopped Fargo in his tracks. She sounded more like a mother than an in-law—or a wife. Even a shrewish wife held her tongue in front of strangers.

"That's all right, ma'am," Fargo said. "Out here on the prairie, I've said worse things myself."

"He knows better," she said tartly. Then Susanna bit her lower lip and sucked in a deep breath when she realized the implied criticism of Fargo and his habits. "I apologize. I didn't mean it that way. It's just that we've had so much trouble getting this far."

"No need to apologize," Fargo said, meaning it. Seeing the rise and fall of her full breasts under the once-white but now dusty blouse was reward enough for him. He hadn't seen another human outside of Parson and his filthy freighters since they'd left Kansas City. Susanna Grafton was a vision of elegant femininity and even better than a long, cold beer for raising his spirits.

Fargo circled the two men who warily watched him as if he would jump them at any instant. The left rear wagon wheel had lost two spokes.

"If you tried driving much farther like that, you'd break the wheel," he said.

"Can you fix it?"

"If you can get the wheel off and have a couple spare spokes, it won't take more than an hour." Fargo looked up into the twilight and saw the evening star winking down at him. He knew better than to make a wish on it. Susanna Grafton was already hitched, probably to Ben Grafton. That didn't dampen his desire to help them, though. Fargo saw they were rank greenhorns and needed to be shown how to do the most elementary repairs on their wagon.

"How'd you get this far without breaking a spoke or wheel?" he asked, grunting as he helped Zeb lever the wagon up so Ben could remove the wheel.

"We've been lucky," Zeb said. The young man carried a powerful lot of suspicion that Fargo had no desire to deal with at the moment. Ben dropped a couple new spokes to the ground by him, along with tools.

"Thanks," Fargo said dryly, setting to work getting the iron wheel rim off so he could replace the busted spokes.

"We . . . we can't pay you for your work," Susanna said anxiously, moving hesitantly toward him as if he were a raging fire and she was both cold and afraid of burning up.

"I'm not looking to get paid," Fargo said. "This is the neighborly thing to do. Where are you folks from?"

"St. Louis," Susanna said, ignoring both men's gestures to keep quiet. "We've been on the trail to Denver City for so long it seems like this is all we've ever known. It gets so lonely out here."

"At least you've got scouts to break the monotony," Fargo said, hammering the second spoke into place and fitting the iron rim back on.

"Scouts? I don't know what you mean. There's just us," Susanna said.

"Hush your mouth," snapped Ben. He took the shotgun from Zeb's hands and pointed it toward Fargo. "He's fixin' to rob us. That's why he's askin' all them questions."

"You want to lift the wagon so I can work the wheel back on or do you want to do it yourselves?" Fargo asked. He dusted off his hands, stared at Ben and the shotgun clutched in his shaking hands. "Good luck and good evening. Ma'am," Fargo said, touching the brim of his hat in Susanna's direction.

"Wait, don't be offended. Ben's just edgy. What men are you talking about?"

"I came on your tracks down in yonder wash. Following your trail, maybe an hour behind, were at least three riders. When you got out of the ravine, they set off for other parts."

"We don't know who they might be," Susanna said.

"He's lying," Zeb said. "He wants to spook us."

"This isn't St. Louis," Fargo said. "If I wanted to spook you, I'd mention that you're standing right next to a prairie rattler about ready to sink its fangs into your leg."

Zeb jumped a foot, wildly looking around. Fargo smiled without any humor at his small practical joke. They were all tenderfeet and had no business being on the trail alone.

"Maybe I'll see you in Denver," Fargo said, going to his Ovaro and getting ready to mount.

"Wait, Mr. Fargo, don't go like this. I am so sorry. I apologize for—"

"Don't do it, Susanna," snapped Ben. "Let him go."

"He helped us. We'd be stuck out here for days until you two figured how to fix that wheel. The least we can do is give him a decent meal."

Fargo's mouth began to water at the thought of something more than beans and salty buffalo jerky for dinner. Clem Parson had not hired on any muleteer worthy of being called a cook. Chuck with the freighters was always stomach-turningly similarly to their prior meal, except when Fargo took time to hunt pheasant or rabbit along the way.

"Let him get on his way," chimed in Zeb. "We don't want to hold him up."

Fargo climbed into the saddle and stared down at Susanna Grafton. She was a lovely woman and angry at the way her husband and brother-in-law had treated him. Fargo knew better than to get involved in a family squabble. Whatever spooked the men was something they had to work out among themselves.

"Good evening," he said, turning to go. He halted, then stood in the stirrups as he stared into the dying last rays of light sneaking between the sharp peaks of the distant Rocky Mountains.

"What is it, Mr. Fargo?"

"You say you didn't have anyone scouting for you?"

"Why, no, no one at all. We couldn't afford it."

"There are five men riding mighty fast in this direction." Fargo's mind raced. If the three he had followed circled around to the west, they could have joined up with the other pair and waited for the Grafton wagon to rattle along. When it never appeared, the five men might have come looking for it. If so, Fargo knew their reasons for seeking out the Graftons weren't too peaceable or law-abiding.

"Robbers!" cried Zeb trying to grab the shotgun from Ben's hands.

"What do you think, Mr. Fargo?" asked Susanna. Her stricken expression would have held him here to defend the three greenhorns, even if his common decency had not been enough.

"I think he's right," Fargo said. "Can you hold them off?"

"Shoot them?" asked Zeb. "Yes!"

"Get to it," Fargo said. "If you have another gun, use it." His lake-blue eyes speared Ben Grafton.

"I don't know where it is," Ben stammered, flustered at the sudden turn of events.

"I do," Susanna said, pushing past him and rooting around in the wagon like a prairie dog digging its burrow. She came out with a small-caliber Smith & Wesson.

"Wait until they get closer, then start firing," ordered Fargo.

"Where are you going?" asked Susanna, seeing him turn his horse's face away from them.

"He's leaving us to be killed. He's a coward!" cried Ben.

Fargo wanted to hit the man for such a lie but had no time. If his hastily contrived plan was to work, he had to ride—fast. Leaving the three behind and letting them think he was a lily-livered coward rankled Fargo but he knew staying to explain to them was not an option.

The first sharp crack of gunshot echoed in the still evening air. From the sound, Fargo knew the approaching riders had opened fire. The report was nothing like what a shotgun or a revolver would make. He galloped until he got into a shallow ravine, cut north for a hundred yards, then urged the Ovaro up the steep cutbank and westward, setting up a one-man ambush from behind.

If he caught the outlaws, he might confuse them and make them think they had ridden into a trap where they were out-numbered and outgunned. Of course he would need the Graftons to open fire to pull it off.

Fargo cut another sharp corner and headed back south, hidden in the dust cloud kicked up by the five galloping outlaws. He barely made out their silhouettes as they shouted and fired wildly at the wagon, not intending to hit any of the Graftons but wanting only to scare them into surrendering.

If the pilgrims did surrender, Fargo knew they were lost. They had to put up a fight or the road agents would have hostages Fargo could never free.

As he prepared to lose both the men and the lovely Susanna, he heard the sharp crack of a shotgun followed quickly by the duller snap of the six-shooter firing repeatedly. This was enough to force the road agents to slow their all-out attack and cluster together to rethink their assault. Fargo drew his Henry from its saddle sheath and levered in a round. He drew his Colt and used his knees to guide the Ovaro as it raced toward the outlaws.

Shouting like an attacking Cheyenne, Fargo began firing, the rifle in his left hand and the six-gun in his right. When the six-shooter came up empty he used both hands on the Henry for a more accurate shot. To his relief, he heard more shots fired from the direction of the Grafton wagon.

Fargo hoped the highwaymen would break off their attack and hightail it quick. His Colt was empty and his Henry's magazine was getting perilously close to being exhausted. With only a round or two left in the rifle, Fargo saw the road agents make up their minds.

They ran like scalded dogs, leaving behind the wagon they had thought to be easy prey.

Slowing his headlong gallop, Fargo emerged from the dust cloud. He worried the Graftons would mistake him for one of the outlaws—or not care.

Ben jumped up, and took careful aim with his Smith & Wesson. Susanna cried out to stop, but Ben pulled the trigger. From a dozen yards away, Fargo heard the hammer fall on the empty cylinder. Never had a sound been so welcome.

Fargo rode more slowly, giving Susanna the chance to grab the pistol from her husband's grip.

'They're gone," Fargo said. "From the way they were riding, I don't think they'll be back any time soon."

"But you don't know?" Susanna asked anxiously.

"Ma'am, I can't rightly say. It's unusual seeing a gang attack a single wagon. They might go after a stage, but this is off the regular route into Denver City and frankly, there's not a whole lot you'd be carrying that would appeal to them." He eyed her significantly, letting Susanna finish his thought. Material goods like furniture and plow blades might not be what a road agent desired most, but a fine looking doe like Susanna Grafton certainly was.

"Do you think they follows us?" Zeb asked.

"From St. Louis?" Fargo scoffed at Zeb's notion that they were that important. "I suspect the gang was riding along and saw easy pickings."

"We're not that easy to kill!" protested Ben. Susanna silenced him with a cold look.

"No, I can see that you're not," Fargo said, pouring a drop of oil on stormy water. He heaved a deep sigh and knew what he had to do with them. Leaving them to their own devices was a surefire way of getting them killed, even if they were only a few days' travel from Denver.

The alternative wouldn't satisfy anyone, but Fargo saw no way around it.